TUMBLING DOWN

a novel by
Billy Roche

TASSEL PUBLICATIONS

BILLY ROCHE'S Tumbling Down was first published by Wolfhound Press in 1986. His first stage play, A Handful Of Stars, was staged at The Bush Theatre in 1988. This was followed by Poor Beast In The Rain in 1990. Belfry completed this powerful trilogy at the Bush Theatre. All three plays, directed by Robin LeFevre, became known as The Wexford Trilogy and were performed in their entirety at The Bush, the Peacock and the Theatre Royal, Wexford. Later The Wexford Trilogy was filmed for the B.B.C., directed by the late, great Stuart Burge. His fourth play Amphibians was commissioned by the R.S.C. and performed at the Barbican. This was followed by The Cavalcaders at The Peacock and Royal Court, London. He wrote the screenplay for Trojan Eddie, which was directed by Gillies MacKinnon and starred Stephen Rea and Richard Harris. Trojan Eddie won the Best Film Award at The San Sebastian Film Festival in 1996. His sixth play On Such As We was performed at the Peacock in 2001, directed by Wilson Milam and starring Brendan Gleeson. Billy has been Writer-In-Residence at the Bush and Writer-In-Association at Druid and the Abbey Theatre. Tales From Rainwater Pond, a collection of short stories, was published by Pillar Press in 2006

Praise for *Tumbling Down*

"What makes this book so exceptional is the sheer quality of the writing...pause and savour its felicities"
Gerry Colgan (The Irish Independent.)

"Tumbling Down is...Dubliners with the comic gusto of Damon Runyan"
Irish Times.

"As seductive and brilliant as anything he has written...a luminous and inspirational book"
Conor McPherson.

"A beautifully written true life fairy tale...the reason I'm a writer."
Eoin Colfer.

First published by Wolfhound Press in 1986.
This revised edition published by Tassel Publications in 2008.

Tassel Publications, Wexford.

British Library Cataloguing in Publication Data

A CIP record for this book is available from the British
Library.

ISBN 978-0-9559154-0-6

Design & Typesetting: Blue Ark Design Ltd.
Illustrations by Fionnuala McMullin
Printed by Betaprint Ltd., Dublin 12.

To my wife, Patti

In memory of May and Pierce & Jack and Kitty.

CHAPTER ONE

Captain Crunch strolled up the quay, looking like something from a Bogart movie – the black coat with the collar turned up and the hand stuffed into his pocket as if it was caressing the trigger of a gun. The morning frost tingled unthawed on the Woodenworks and far away a chapel bell donged out a funeral lament as a little procession of old men and women toddled home from ten mass. A bunch of men on the dole stood on the street corner debating the day's racing form while a uniformed postman glided effortlessly by on his bicycle, sweetly whistling *Carolina Moon*. The smoke from the gas works curled up in the shape of Scandinavia and disappeared into the atmosphere. Wexford, a topsy-turvy town that rose up and tumbled down into rows and rows of gardenless houses, streets filled with people whose main ambition was to live until they died.

Crunch glanced across at the half-dead harbour and softly sighed: once it was filled with ships and sailors, stevedores and dockers and wheelers; now it could just about muster the strength to feed the handful of fishermen who ploughed the seabed day in and day out for mussels. Useless Island stood alone and unused in the middle of this shipless harbour, an island of stone and clay that looked like it must have sprung from the sea centuries ago. Crunch's eyes avoided it. The gulls did too. Even the fishermen stayed well clear of it and the absence of life lent the place a ghostly, enchanted air.

Before him the bridge leapfrogged across the river, like a sly fugitive tiptoeing out of town. Pigeons cooed, '*look at the fool*,' from on high and the dismal harbour bars and cheap boarding houses held no solace either. Up Cinema Lane and a million boyhood memories gnawed at his heart - memories of jeering and duelling and cowboys crossing rivers. But no sooner had he left the clapped-out cinema behind than he forgot about it, because, '*that was then and this is now, Sugar.*'

A gust of icy wind came stealing in from the sea, causing his pants to flutter and puffing his threadbare coat up like a parachute. Some woman's hat was whisked off her head and went sailing helter-skelter down the street without her. A passing window cleaner had to lay his heavy ladder up against a wall and run after it for her. Crunch brushed heedlessly by: he was alone now, alone and forsaken in a hostile land, a parched and forgotten man.

'A friggin' ghost town,' Crunch couldn't help thinking as he strode. 'All that's lacking are a couple of tumbleweeds rolling up the street and Audie Murphy riding in from the other side to gun El Cruncho down.' No need to bother: if Crunch didn't get a drink soon he'd dry up and wither with the drought.

Main Street was only wiping the sleep from its eyes, yawning and blinking. Scarfed and rosy women stood tattling and gawking or went scuttling from shop to shop. On this narrow, twisting, Viking street, the traffic, with scarcely room to budge, stuttered and crawled to a standstill. Meanwhile, Victor, the town's village idiot, stood mid-stream, accusing, conducting and directing. A messenger boy scooped his big bicycle around him with the skill of an equestrian and frantically pedalled onwards, singing *The Hucklebuck* at the top of his cheap, melodious voice. A wiry delivery man with his railway hat tilted slightly skew-ways on his head commanded his heavy footed dray horse to a halt and manoeuvred out of the jam without a scrape; he clicked his tongue, swished the tinkling reins and grimaced as his sturdy shire cantered on, dragging a big noisy juggernaut of a cart behind him. A dismayed commercial traveller, stuck behind the wheel of his motorcar, threw his hands to heaven in mock surrender, and the antics of Victor - who looked a scarecrow cum tick-tack man - caused the stranger to shake his head in mild disbelief.

Crunch cringed as Wexford beeped and bamped itself alive. He dodged people he didn't want to meet, pretending not to notice them and disregarding their hellos. And fairly soon he was where he wanted to be: in The Bullring and standing outside Johnny's tiny Shoebox. Johnny might be good for the loan of a few quid, worth a shot anyway. But the shop was closed and partially shuttered. Crunch tried the door, shaking it venomously and cursing out loud. He stood on his tippy toes and peeped through the top pane of the window. The mended shoes were carefully labelled and parcelled in brown paper and stacked on spotless shelves behind the counter, while the damaged ones were tagged and piled in a forlorn heap by the door. Yesterday's paper was spread out on the warped wooden bench at the back wall, and Johnny's tools were either lying or hanging where they were supposed to be. The cat was outside on the window sill and the floor was swept and an immaculate blue apron was draped carelessly across the vacant working chair. The only missing ingredient was the man in question.

'He must be on the ran-tan,' Crunch concluded, vainly trying the door one more time. And then he turned to behold Ned Stand's enormous face staring out at him from beneath the awning of his dowdy pawnshop, the cloying stench of misfortune seeping from within.

Ned flashed his gold-toothed smirk, which Crunch instinctively aped (like two silent clowns in a make believe mirror). There was no love lost between this duo, everyone knew that. Ned, who took pride in the fact that he could bamboozle the best of them, would not forget in a hurry that Crunch had once sold him a bicycle he already owned. It'd been parked outside and marked *'For Sale'*. Crunch just wheeled it in, got thirty shillings for it and skedaddled. Ned soon twigged it naturally enough and vowed someday to have his revenge, and now he practically prickled with glee as his poor down-in-the-mouth foe dawdled away.

Crunch scurried out of sight and veered down a side street and onto the quay again, arriving outside The Shamrock Bar where he searched his pockets yet again for a ray of hope – top pocket, inside pocket, lining and everywhere: no, nothing doing. And as he paced up and down like a muttering madman, he kept one eye peeled for some familiar face, someone who might save the day. All he needed was the entrance fee, the price of a stout. Jesus Christ tonight, was that too much to ask for? And then he thought he heard the sound of singing coming from the pub. Well, music definitely! And laughter! Yes, joyous laughter, followed by mysterious stretches of prolonged, bewitching silence. 'Oh, Jesus, Mary and Joseph,' someone heard him say.

The Shamrock was a tall, lean, drunken building with crumbling walls and moss-filled chutes. The sign overhead had a 'T' missing and the 'R' was slantways. It leaned against The Small Hotel, a well-ordered old-fashioned place with polished knockers and shining silverware. A glass canopy spread itself out over the pavement with '*The Small Hotel*' spelt out in proud, bold lettering on all three sides. These two establishments were as disparate as chalk and cheese and yet they huddled together like two lost orphans in a storm, urging each other on from day to day.

Inside The Shamrock had not got much to offer in the way of decoration. The ground floor was a cosy bar with a fine mirror etched in the shape of a shamrock. There was a huge thick counter, originally intended for a bank (or so it goes), and many stories were told by the old drinkers recalling the day it was installed and the hardship of the job. A snug, not much bigger than a confession box, faced out onto the waterfront, and hanging on the walls were flags and pennants and souvenirs from every port in the world, all brought back by the many deep-sea sailors who frequented the place. There was a long peculiar-shaped bamboo pipe, supposedly to have come from some Oriental opium den, and on the wall opposite the bar a colourful Chinese fan was opened out. Sometimes a false newspaper report, depicting one of the boys in some compromising position abroad, would find its way home. This would be given pride of place on the wall and it would remain there until it became stained with smoke and brittle with deterioration or until everyone got fed up of the story. A long soft seat arched along one wall, reserved for any women who might drop in. Down below you'd find the *'Gents'* and a dark hole of a cellar where cobwebs dangled from the ceiling and fungus sprouted from the ancient walls. Upstairs were the **'Ladies'** and a silent, seldom-used lounge (weddings, wakes and small reunions). Here an old, ghosty piano sat like a jilted lover, waiting patiently for the past. On the third floor there were two dusty storerooms, haphazardly packed with all sorts of useless junk that nobody had the heart to throw out: a broken-down cash register, old newspapers, unpaid bills, grey photographs, off-the-market drinks, cardboard boxes full of corks and labels and queer looking corkscrews. And this was The Shamrock, ramshackle and rickety from stern to bow, but of course to Crunch, who was stranded on the outside, it was a well-rigged raft that was bound for bluer and calmer waters.

He surveyed the cloudy sky now, already spitting a hint of rain, and he conjured from his top pocket the butt of a cigarette so small that he wondered why he ever bothered to save it in the first place. He lit up, striking his last fluffy match off the wall and cupping his hands together for protection. Successful, he puffed a few wisps of smoke out and up to be blown away as a hail of dewy drops landed on and trickled down his bleary-eyed face.

It began to shower, a sudden soft downpour, and, muffling up, he stepped into the relative comfort of The Small Hotel porch. And, as he gazed out from behind the curtain of rain that dripped from the canopy, he frisked his past and tried to recall the legion of great strokes he must have pulled in his heyday: maybe there he might find some magic sesame that would open that forbidden door.

The commercial traveller pulled up in front of the Small Hotel, got out and hurried inside, and before long the baby-faced bellboy arrived to retrieve his luggage from the booth of his lime green motor car, hotel umbrella at hand (*The Small Hotel* in roundy writing). Crunch sucked the last drag from the scut, spat out the loose tobacco that had gathered around his lips and tossed the fag-end away; it landed in a puddle and went out with a hiss. And that's when he summoned up the courage to do what had to be done: he stepped out into the elements, adopted a hangdog expression and hunched his way into the bar.

Crunch faltered on the threshold to take stock. A young sailor was surrounded by a bunch of scavengers who were clearly out to soak him dry. One of them- Lar Lyons- passed some remark, which Crunch didn't even bother to acknowledge. Down in the corner by the dartboard Joe Crofton had his nose stuck into the racing page. He was wearing glasses and looked older and more civilised than usual. Timmy Flynn, alias Forty Winks, had made a pillow out of his elbows and had settled down for a delicious snooze on the counter. Johnny was there too, whistling softly through his teeth and smoking a Tom Thumb cigar, smoke curling up in curlicues all around him.

Seventeen year old Davy Wolfe- me that is- sat on a high stool behind the bar with my feet cocked up on the counter, picking my battered old guitar. I knew that Crunch was flat broke and I played on it. I knew from his submissive stance and the caution in his step. If Crunch had any money he would have bellowed at me by now to cut out the racket and get him a drink. I strummed the strings, rising to a noisy crescendo, so that in the end half the place turned to look at me – Johnny with amused upturned eyebrows and Joe Crofton peering out over his glasses like some piqued professor. Crunch, in the meantime, was putting on a show of his own – licking his lips and shaking his head and grimacing. I put down my instrument carefully and turned to wonder what I could do for him.

'A large bottle,' he barked, and motioned with his thumb and forefinger that a drop of whiskey was also in order.

Someone launched into a song and he winced. The singer sounded so bad that even Forty Winks surfaced and wondered about it.

'Let it be written,' Crunch said, casting a furtive glance over his shoulder.

I Never Dream
But When I Dream Of You.
I Love You As I've Never Loved Before ....

'How's the Captain?' Johnny hailed from the far end of the counter.

Crunch indicated that he had seen better times and Johnny smiled sympathetically as the grizzled old sea-dog bowed his head in search of solitude.

Johnny was a warm-hearted character with the weary aura of a fallen angel. He stood five feet nothing and had soft wavy hair and a fascinating face. His nose was of the stodgy breed (from a row with a lamppost) and his eyes were sad and sincere and wonderful. From a mouthful of snow white teeth poured a husky velvet voice that would put you in mind of Mel Torme. He dressed impeccably too with freshly starched shirts and Fred-Astaire-style suits, two-toned shoes and bow ties to match. And his stance was casual and relaxed, especially when he sang: he'd plunge one hand into his baggy pants-pocket and croon out some old Bing Crosby number or fall down on one knee and warble like Al Jolson. Johnny was forever singing; if he got tired singing he'd hum; if he was too hoarse to hum he'd whistle. He was whistling now, whistling and smiling. *When The Red Red Robin/ Goes Bob Bob Bobbin' Along...*

> *When You Were Sweet* (the others bawled)
> *When You Were Sweet..... Sixteen...*

The young sailor bought Crunch a large bottle and tipped him a conspiratorial wink. Crunch welcomed the drink, it goes without saying, and - to his credit (well in his view anyway) - he resisted the selfish urge to pipe the smirking greenhorn aboard.

'Hey Johnny, that reminds me, Easy Goin' Larry is lookin' for you,' Crunch eventually said as he poured, nearly having to shout over the commotion.

'He's lookin' for me? Where is he?' Johnny wondered.

'He's down in the Bullring. The man is walkin' around in his stocking feet. Says he to me, "If you see that other fella you might tell him I'm wantin' me shoes back,"' and Crunch sort of painfully scoffed as he said it.

'Was he down there though?' Johnny queried, his face creased with concern all of a sudden.

'Naw, I'm only jokin' you,' Crunch reassured him, forcing a yawn. 'He told me you had a pair of boots belongin' to him alright!'

'I have, yeah. A right pair of boots they are too. I must have a look at them when I go back,' and with that Johnny doused his stumpy butt in the slender lid of his empty cigar tin.

'He told me he got *Rabbit Skin* good for the two-thirty,' Crunch told him out of the side of his mouth.

'Yeah, I know. He gave it to me too, sure, the other day…No chance! What's Wooden Arse ridin' in the two-thirty, Joe? *Plug* is it?'

'What? Yeah … *Plug*. He should walk away with it,' Joe Crofton decreed without looking up.

'Easy Goin' Larry said that *Rabbit Skin* was good for that race,' Johnny teased and winked at me.

Joe Crofton took off his glasses, sat back on his stool and stretched. 'I'd be inclined to go with Wooden Arse Clampton all the way today. *Plug*, *Charlie Boy* and *Tailor's Hall*,' he said. 'Give us another drink here, Davy when you're ready…. And twenty fags too.'

'Let's have a look at that paper, Joe,' Johnny said, reaching across.

The song had fizzled out and the scavengers were toying with a few more ideas, singing a few annoying lines of this song and a bar or two of another.

'Hey Crofton, what do you think of the lad here?' the sleeveen Lar Lyons said then out of the blue, referring to the young sailor.

'What about him?' Joe Crofton said, fearing the worst.

'I believe he got word when he was at sea that his aul' granny was dead - nearly ninety years of age - and do you know what he did when he heard the news? What are you blushin' for, boy? Look at him, lads. He's gone as red as anything.'

'Give us a loan of a pen, Davy,' Johnny interrupted and accepted the pen that Joe Crofton held out to him.

'Do you know what he did though, Joe?' Lar Lyons persisted. 'Give one guess what he did, boy.'

Joe Crofton appeared to give the matter some thought, rubbing his tired eyes and clearing his throat before turning to face Lar Lyons head on. 'I don't know,' he said. 'He cried, I suppose,' he guessed, and Lar Lyons didn't know what to say then or where to look.

At twelve o'clock the angelus bell rang and, as if in protest, the young sailor got sick all over his shoes on the last few strokes. The lads on either side of him nearly wrecked the place trying to get clear of him – a stool overturned and a table upended. My father, who was working below in the yard, came up with a face of vengeance on him and ran the whole lot of them out of it, Lar Lyons stepping slyly aside to distance himself from it all.

'Bloody jowlsters,' my father said, and he cast me a murderous look as if it was half my fault. Rain dripped from his hair down onto his crimson face and the big flapping Wellington boots that he wore left behind a trail of dirty footprints in his wake.

'I thought it was **The Creature From The Black Lagoon** there for a minute,' Crunch joked when he was gone.

'Hey Crunch, you might clean that up for us there,' I pleaded, handing him the mop.

'What? Go and play with yourself somewhere,' he said and turned his back on me.

'Aw go on out of that.'

'No.'

'No?'

'Davy Wolfe, will you go away and don't be annoyin' me. I haven't the stomach for that kind of thing.'

'Aw, have a heart Crunch, it won't take you a minute,' I begged and I pestered him to take the mop from me.

'If you don't go away out of that I'll give you the greatest box in the forehead you ever got,' he snarled, and he threw me a crooked, comical glare.

I mopped up the first layer of vomit with some newspaper and as I passed by I taunted him with it. 'Mooah...' I said.

'Ain't that fuckin' awful,' he growled, standing up. 'A man can't even have a drink in peace anymore without...' and I tossed my head back and laughed my way out to the dustbin.

I was the first to go for lunch that day and by the time I got back Crunch was rejuvenated. He called for a large bottle and paid for it, leading me to presume that he must have put the hammer on Johnny for a few quid while I was gone.

'If the Smithwicks crowd call, Davy, tell them I'm wantin' two barrels of Guinness and one Harp,' my father informed me as he climbed into his topcoat.

'Right,' I said and began tinkering around with my guitar again.

'And listen, tell them there's a rake of empties out in the laneway,' he added from the doorway. 'The key of the wicket-gate is up there in the silver mug, the one with the handle there. I'll see ye after lads,' and he coughed his way onto the street.

'Good luck Paddy,' Johnny called after him and Joe Crofton mumbled, 'All the best,' when he heard the door slam.

The men smoked and drank in silence as I fiddled about with *Brother Can You Spare A Dime*, Johnny urging me on with his eyes, adding an odd husky word here and there. Forty Winks stirred and came up for air, swore and slipped back to sleep again.

'You're after wakin' the child,' Johnny chastised, his finger to his lips.

I smiled, stopped playing and surrendered.

'Give us over that racin' pad there, Davy,' Johnny said then, jotting down his bet and sliding it towards me with a grateful grin.

'Turn on the telly before you go there, Davy' Joe Crofton called.

I obliged and then I raced like an emissary up to the betting shop where an unshaven character with a pencil behind his ear confidentially confided in me that **Regal Prince** was a dead cert for the three o'clock. I caught a glimpse of his own docket on my way out and noticed that he was backing **Stately Homes** in the race himself. How could you be up to them?

I tramped back down to the pub and by the time I got there the race was over and done with. *Plug* was down the field and Joe Crofton looked positively cheesed off. *Rabbit Skin* had walked away with it and not even Johnny could see the funny side of it. Crunch clattered all the small change he had left up onto the counter and told me to pick out a horse. I glanced at the paper and just took a chance.

'*Caribbean Sunset*,' I said.

Crunch's face dropped as he spied Joe Crofton shake his enlightened head in the mirror.

'He'll leave them all standing,' I assured him as I scooped up his money.

Crunch made a feeble attempt to get me to change my mind, but I wrote it down anyway and in the end he reluctantly agreed to it. Johnny said he thought Wooden Arse was off form today and he backed *Dirty Harry*. Joe Crofton argued that *Charlie Boy* couldn't be beaten and it wouldn't matter who was riding him. He said you could put Gordon Glynt up on him and he'd still run away with the race.

'Timmy, are you wantin' to back anything?' Joe Crofton said, nudging a snoozing, snoring Forty Winks.

Forty Winks stirred and peeped out. '*Caribbean Sunset*,' he bleated and slipped back to sleep again.

A scowling Joe Crofton looked my way. Johnny, tittering, extracted a crinkled pound note from Forty Winks' top pocket while Joe Crofton scribbled down his bet.

'Bring down another pad when you're comin' back, Davy. That one is nearly done-for,' Johnny suggested as I made individual parcels out of the four bets, wrapping the money up inside each docket.

'Right,' I promised and hurried back up to the betting shop again.

The unshaven character with the pencil behind his ear was still hanging around there, like it was his second home. He regarded me suspiciously as I burrowed my way through the huddled conclave of men that had gathered around the counter, their faces grave and concerned as they listened with tilted heads to a crackly old speaker.

'Six-to-one,' someone said. 'That was a turn up for the books alright,'

'Wooden Arse Clampton should be shot to death with balls of his own shit, that's all,' the unshaven character with the pencil behind his ear proclaimed and no one disagreed. Except the woman behind the counter that is who allowed a disapproving sound to slip out as she stamped my dockets and doled out my change.

When I got back to The Shamrock the horses were down at the starting post and ready for the off. The commentator, when speaking about *Caribbean Sunset*, said, *'This old-trooper may find it rough going here today,'* and Crunch, like an overheated engine, exhaled a geezer of air down through his nose and out through his mouth simultaneously.

'And they're off. First out of the box is Dirty Harry followed by Regal Prince and Stately Homes with Charlie Boy and The Serpent in hot pursuit. Summertime Blues, The Downer and Shenandoah, The Lady Is A Tramp, Hero and bringing up the rear is Caribbean Sunset. And Stately Homes takes the lead with The Serpent in second place, followed by The Downer, Charlie Boy, Dirty Harry, Regal Prince, Summertime Blues, Shenandoah, The Lady Is A Tramp, Hero and Caribbean Sunset.'

Crunch groaned miserably and buried his head in his hands. Before long though *Caribbean Sunset* began to make a bit of ground, passing out *Shenandoah* and *Hero* and I gave Crunch the thumbs up and pretended to ride my stool like a horse, slapping my side and what-not.

'The two behind him must be on crutches,' Crunch moaned, turning his back to the race.

Then, coming to the last two furlongs, Wooden Arse Clampton stood up in the saddle and used his whip for the first time as a brave band of five or six horses broke away from the rest of the pack and good old *Caribbean Sunset* was among them.

'We're inside the last two furlongs now and Charlie Boy has moved up into the lead. Next is The Serpent, Dirty Harry, Stately Homes, The Downer and Caribbean Sunset, and this wee band has branched off from the rest of the field. And what an exciting finish this is going to be with Caribbean Sunset leaving The Downer behind and I think Stately Homes is weakening too. Yes she is and Caribbean Sunset has moved up into third place ... '

Crunch had started to take an interest in the race now, moving closer to the television and hushing people with his raised, upturned hand even though nobody was actually saying anything. Joe Crofton was on his feet too, egging on Charlie boy.

'*And Charlie Boy piles on the pressure, Clampton glancing over his shoulder there and I think he's about to make a break for it. Yes, there he goes and Caribbean Sunset goes with him, tearing up along the outside with an amazing spurt and WHAT A HUMDINGER ... OF ... A ... FINISH ... THIS IS ... GOING ... TO ... BE...And they're neck and neck as they come to the post and this is going to be close. A photo finish ... No no no ... for my money Caribbean Sunset has just scraped it at the post. WHAT A TURN UP FOR THE BOOKS ... WHAT AN AMAZING TURN UP FOR THE BOOKS ... I DON'T BELIEVE IT ... I CAN'T BELIEVE IT .... '*

Crunch was charmed and rolled his tongue around in his mouth as if it was all his idea in the first place. Joe Crofton was disgusted. He pucked Forty Winks and told him to cut out the racket.

'*Yes, winner alright. And we'll have the starting prices for you in just a moment. What a peculiar day's racing we're having here today. It's a bookie's paradise down there ...*'

Hey, what did I tell you,' I said to Crunch and he silenced me as the starting prices appeared on the screen. *Caribbean Sunset* came in at 15 to 1. Hearing this, Crunch started to laugh and I started to laugh and between the two of us we woke up a beaming Forty Winks who must have heard the race in his sleep.

All in all our winnings came to five pounds five and a tanner, a tidy enough sum to possess on a wet Wednesday afternoon. My father came back from lunch, hung his drenched overcoat on a radiator and told me to go off for a few hours. He agreed with the others that Wooden Arse Clampton's performance today was a disgrace and added that he must have dutch elm disease.

'I gave you Rabbit Skin this mornin',' Crunch reminded them. 'None of you would even listen to me.'

'Sure you had no place to keep him, that right Paddy?' Johnny said.

'No, sure the yard is full, Crunch,' my father apologised.

Crunch turned away, feigning indignation.

'Well, I'm goin' to stick with Clampton for the next one anyway,' Joe Crofton insisted. 'Dutch elm disease or mahogany piles!'

Johnny shook his head in disagreement. 'He's way off form, Joe,' he said.

'If Tailor's Hall don't walk away with the next one,' Joe Crofton threatened en route to the toilet, 'I'll take the fuckin' pledge.'

'Easy Joe,' my father cried. 'Easy!'

'Yeah, there's no need for that now,' Johnny playfully called after him as Joe Crofton descended the steep stairs to the basement.

I was buttoning up my handsome short Mod overcoat (which my father called a bum-freezer) and listening to the men debating. The next few hours I would spend in Nolan's Cafe glued to the jukebox. The Small Faces were on it, singing *Sha La La La Lee* and *Somebody Help Me* by the Spencer Davis Group, and Otis Redding singing *My Girl* and *Daydream* by the Lovin' Spoonful, which I had just figured out how to play on the guitar. C to A7th to D7th to G7th. *What A Day For A Daydream/ What A Day For A Daydreamin' Boy...*

'Davy, go up and collect on that docket,' Crunch whispered, leaning forward. 'I'll meet you outside the bookies in a few minutes. We'll go for a bit of a stroll.'

'You won't be strollin' too far in that,' my father muttered, his head in the newspaper.

'Why, is it still rainin' out, Paddy?' Johnny wondered.

'Yes it is. It's spillin',' my father said. 'Davy, open up that wicket gate there, here's the lads,' and the shape of a big lorry darkened the frosted doorway.

I picked up the key and made a mad dash for it. I opened up the wicket gate, handed the lorry driver the key, told him what we wanted and scarpered, leaving him and his sidekick there, humping the heavy barrels down onto a dirty red cushion.

The unshaven character with the pencil behind his ear was standing outside the betting shop when I got there.

'Any joy?' I asked as I slipped by and he shook his head dolefully.

By the time Crunch arrived on the scene I had collected our winnings and was talking to the unshaven character with the pencil behind his ear, boasting about our windfall. Crunch reared up on me when he got me to himself.

'Look, if you're goin' to gab to every Tom, Dick and Harry and let the whole world know that we've a few bob to spare, you can give me my share here and now and scram,' he harangued as we strolled towards the nearest watering hole.

I was only seventeen and small for my age and this caused the barman to approach us with suspicion.

'It's alright, he's with me,' Crunch said, vouching for me.

'I know,' the barman countered. 'That's what I'm worried about.'

I had to settle for an orange juice while Crunch treated himself to a small whisky and a large bottle. I paid for it out of the winnings and then proceeded to count the rest out on the counter.

'You hang on to it, Davy,' Crunch suggested, reasonably. 'I'll only spend it…. Give us twenty fags there too,' he called out. 'Pay the man.'

'We'll divide it up and you can pay him yourself,' I said, spotting the con.

'No no no,' he argued. 'It's better this way.'

'Yeah well you needn't think now that I'm goin' to sit here drinkin' Fanta all day long while you scoff all my hard-earned money,' I told him.

He gave the matter some thought and then he said, 'I know a place. Come on, drink up.'

The Hole In The Wall was a pokey public house just off the quay which gave refuge to secret alcoholics, loose women and under-age delinquents. Crunch said that I fell loosely into the last category. He also informed me that he had a niggling fancy for the woman of the house - a proud looking creature with a magnificent rear. She had a lovely daughter too, no older than myself. I'd often seen her at dances, but I never had the nerve to ask her up. She was slightly taller than me and anyway she seemed to prefer to hang around with the rugby crowd. She came in while we were there, carrying a stupid looking poodle. I blushed as she crossed the room. Crunch took note and proceeded to blow me kisses and imitate her wiggle as he toddled out to the jacks.

We were served by a bandy old man with a grey face and a black shiny suit. When you called for a drink chances were he didn't have it. If he had it he couldn't find it, and even if he did find it he wouldn't know the price of it and he'd have to go fumbling around for a price-list. Crunch called him *Jesse* and sometimes *Mr James*, and the poor devil was terrified of him.

'Mr James, some more tequila for my friend here,' Crunch would bellow and the old man would struggle towards us, holding on to the counter for support.

'What's that?' he'd say. 'The same again is it?' and off he'd go, snooping among the bottles and trembling like a leaf as he poured.

'I'd buy him a drink,' Crunch whispered at one point, 'only I doubt he'd be able for the excitement.'

When Crunch was like this he was great company. I used to love to sit and listen to his yarns about dogs and ferrets and drinking sprees and harmless pranks that went awry; nautical tall tales too of his early days at sea, dangerous stories of blades flashing on the waterfront as two men fought to the death (or near death anyway) down some salty avenue in Amsterdam or somewhere; and beautiful women lapping at his feet on the sunlit shores of Mombassa. In his stories Crunch dealt with pimps, whores and bullyboys with the strength of a Cagney or Gable. All his fables had a frail cabin boy in there somewhere, tagging along blue-eyed behind him (a product of having seen too many John Wayne films I suspect). If and when they reached the whorehouse Crunch would usually relieve the youngster of whatever loot he had in his possession and send him back skulking to the ship.

When Crunch was in his cups he liked to twitter - morbid dirges of mothers' funerals and that kind of thing. His eyes would grow misty and sometimes he would get contrary, particularly if nobody was listening to him. Most of the songs he sang would put years on you, but there was one song in his repertoire that I never grew tired of. It was an old sea ballad called *Malibar:*

Far across the Western ocean
Underneath an Indian star,
Dwelt a dark-eyed young maiden
On the coast of Malibar.

In the harbour where we anchored
I can see her shy and sweet,
With a locket on her bosom
And the white waves at her feet.

Fare thee well my pretty dark eyes
Fare thee well my Indian star,
I will come again and love you
On the coast of Malibar.

Well do I remember
Beneath the palm trees so slim and tall,
Many were the nights I danced with her
In the seaman's mission hall.

Fare thee well my pretty dark eyes
Fare thee well my Indian star,
I will come again and love you
On the coast of Malibar.

It was directly from this song that he invented Indio for me. She was a woman of great savage beauty with jet black hair hanging down onto her shoulders and voluptuous breasts that were permanently swollen with milk. Her teeth were pearls that lit up her face when she spoke and she had legs like pillars and a back so broad that you could nearly play a game of handball up against it. In bed she had the agility of a dancer and her two fiery eyes betrayed a passion that was bordering on insanity.

And as we sat in that footy dark pub on that wet Wednesday afternoon, with Jesse fumbling about and muttering in the background and the sound of agitated voices coming from the living quarters at the rear of the house, I tried to wring the story out of him one more time.

'Tell me about Valparaiso,' I said.

A bewildered look came over him. 'Valparaiso?' he said, rubbing his stubbled chin as if trying to dredge up some vague, distant memory.

'Tell me about Indio,' I urged.

'Indio?' he said, even more mystified.

He had told me this story a thousand times before and always insisted on putting me through this old rigmarole.

'Yeah, tell me about Valparaiso,' I said. 'Tell me about Indio carrying you up to bed and all.'

And he looked at me with fondness, his eyes igniting with importance: yes, it was all coming back to him now alright.

'Valparaiso,' he recalled, giving it some thought. 'A dangerous place I don't mind tellin' you, one hell of a rough place,' he said and he ran an extended finger knife-like across his throat to emphasise his point. 'Pimps, pickpockets and cut-throats waiting to roll the first greenhorn that came ashore,' he warned.

'Did you ever get rolled there?' I foolishly asked.

'Who? The Crunch?' and he shook his head in disbelief: it was a stupid question.

'Did you ever get rolled anywhere?'

'What? Oh yeah, but not there. When I was younger ... greener. ..
I'd wake up in an alley, blood pumpin' out of my head and face and not a penny to my name: watch, ring, wallet and everything - gone! I'd go back to the ship then, all down-hearted. Maybe the boys might chip in and raise a few bob for you, maybe not.'

He shrugged it off and I had a vision of a bruised sad sailor reading a cowboy book in his bunk while all his mates were living it up ashore.

'But not in Valparaiso,' he continued. 'They knew me there you see - on account of Indio,' and here as usual he painted a picture for me of a rope-creaking, bustling seaport with bales of cotton, boxes of coffee and barrels of fruit being shifted and shunted and hoisted about. The dockers, all wearing string vests, are lithe and rhythmic as a sweating fat man with a cigar in his gob bawls out orders at them. And sitting on top of a bale of cotton there's a sleazy looking character in a panama hat, fiddling around with a switch-blade knife and threatening the shoe-shining orphans.

"'Hey El Cruncho, you want for me to find you a woman?" a boy asks, spitting on his rag.

"Presto, presto," Crunch barks back at him and then with urgent clicking fingers he orders the boy to get on with it.

Handsome Santina calls from the hold of a nearby ship, "El Cruncho, Indio waits for you," and Crunch tosses the boy a coin and swaggers bowlegged down the creaky gangplank.

I can see her house too, a falling-down wooden shack with a screen door and a few rickety steps leading up to the porch. The roof of the porch is riddled with holes and the sun filters through, streaming down on a hammock that dangles there. The hammock is in motion, even though there is nobody next or near it. Indio sits on the top step, filing her nails and humming, her brown body glinting like gold in the sun, her long legs sprawled out in front of her, tiny beads of sweat glittering on her sullen brow as she gazes sideways into the sizzling heat haze.

'Aw Davy you should see her, though,' Crunch was saying, bringing me back to the land of the living again. 'She's some woman, boy.'

'Is she big?' I pressed: one of my (and his for that matter) favourite questions.

'Big? She's massive, that's all,' he said, trying desperately to describe her but running out of hands. 'I'll tell you one thing now, she'd be hard set to get through that door there and that's no lie. The big thighs on her!' and he pondered this awhile. 'She'd kill you,' he added, looking me up and down and secretly measuring me with his roving eyes. 'Oh yes, she would. Kill you,' and once again he tried to sculpt her shape out for me with a fluid, moulding motion.

'And she was in love with you?' I said.

He just nodded, 'yes', modesty forbidding him to say any more. Then he took a long slow drag on his cigarette and smiled at the sad realisation that she loved him.

'She used to carry me up the stairs,' he went on. 'On her own now!' he stressed. 'She'd put me lying down on an aul' sofa, and I paralytic drunk. Then she'd look down at me that way,' (here he acted out how she might look at him with lowered eyes and wide open angry nostrils), "El Cruncho Bastardo," she'd say and I'd laugh in my sleep.'

Then the girl came back out to the bar, interrupting our conversation. She was carrying a tray with her dinner on it and a glass of milk. She sat up at the counter with her back to us and said to Jesse, 'You go ahead home now, Michael. I'll look after things here.'

'How is your mammy?' Jesse asked her.

'She's alright,' she said with little or no concern.

'God, I thought she looked terrible shook up there this morning,' Jesse said, reaching for his overcoat.

'She'll be alright before she's twice married, Michael,' she answered through a mouthful of food.

'What? Yeah. Tell her to mind herself anyway,' Jesse said. 'I'll go so, Linda. Goodbye,' and he began to totter towards the front door.

'Goodbye Michael,' she said without even looking round.

'Do you want me to come down in the morning or anything, Linda?' he called from the open doorway.

'What? Oh yeah, you'd better come down anyway, just in case, like.'

Jesse nodded, smiled in our direction and left.

'Watch out for the desperados,' Crunch muttered as the door banged shut.

'What's that?' Linda said, swivelling round.

'I beg your pardon,' Crunch said, craning his neck forward and extending his body towards her.

'Did you say something?'

'No ... no I was just talkin' to ... eh .... How are you keeping?'

'Grand thanks,' Linda said, going back to her food.

'It's quiet enough.'

'What's that?'

'I say it's very quiet,' Crunch called out to her.

'Mmm ... .' she agreed and left it at that, and Crunch, implying that the place was only a dump and that she had well and truly been put her in her place, winked at me victoriously.

There followed a long embarrassing silence then, which made me feel very ill-at-ease: Crunch shouldn't have said that the place was very quiet.

'Give us another drink here please, when you're ready,' I said, just to break the ice.

Linda, taken by surprise, turned around, swallowed a quick gulp of milk and put down her knife and fork with a crash.

'Lord God Almighty,' Crunch gallantly growled, 'can't you see the girl is tryin' to have her dinner.'

'No, that's alright,' she said, sizing up the round and making a move to go behind the counter.' Sure that's what I'm here for...The same again is it?'

'Yeah,' I said. 'Please.'

'Or something similar says you,' she said

'Oh, and a drop of whiskey as well,' Crunch said, standing up and going towards her with his empty tumbler.

'Have a drink yourself too,' I called over to her and Crunch's head whipped around in amazement.

'Oh, thanks very much,' she said without any hesitation. 'I'll just have a gin and tonic, thanks.'

Crunch cast me a sidelong, disapproving glance and slowly shook his head, a sort of a wordless plea for patience I suppose. There was no tonic in the bar and she had to go into the back of the house to fetch some. Crunch pinched a few of her chips while she was gone and walked across to sit down again.

'Here, put that on the counter there for her,' I said, handing him a pound note.

He took it from me and left it on the counter, nicking another chip and remarking to no one in particular, 'They're grand.'

Linda had left the door to the living-quarters ajar and we could hear herself and her mother bickering about something or other in there. Linda called her mother a silly cow and her mother said that she

21

was nothing only a little bitch going around. Linda came storming out then with a furious face on her, slamming the door behind her.

'That one's a right little anti-Christ, I'd say,' Crunch mumbled as she stood calculating by the till.

She seemed to suspect that one of us had been at her chips. I tried to look and act nonchalant but I could feel my face going red as she glared across at us.

'How much have we left?' Crunch wanted to know, immune to her suspicion.

'I don't know.'

'Check how much we have there.'

'No, we'll check afterwards,' I said, not wanting to make a holy show of myself counting out money like a miser in front of her.

The poodle waddled out and started sniffing around at our table, brushing against our feet and cocking her leg and that. Up close it was a fairly mangy brute with matted hair and bald patches all over it. Crunch said that it resembled Linda's runaway da who he said was nothing only a balding little nettle too.

'Get out be fucked,' Crunch thundered when the dog growled at him and he hit it a sideswipe with his foot. 'I hate them yokes,' he confessed.

Soon after that we decided to call it a day. I had to go back to work that night and I wanted to go up home and have my tea first. I smiled at Linda as we left, hoping that maybe the next time we met at a dance or somewhere she might remember me and not just look through me like she usually did.

Outside we muffled ourselves up and stood to consider our alternatives: north or south? It had stopped raining and the street looked silvery and sad. Across the road, standing in the mouth of Roman Lane, Victor stood with his arms akimbo. He looked pleased as the free flowing traffic slipped on by. A street sweeper pushed his broom and barrow, tut-tutting at the shards of manure the galloping railway horse had left behind. The commercial traveller, taking a stroll, smiled at Victor who grinned, frowned and laughed all in one fell swoop.

'He's not half as mad as he lets on to be,' Crunch told me confidentially as Victor traced the wary stranger's footsteps. And then with a sudden theatrical flourish Crunch waved us both out of there. 'Here,' he said, 'Come on, let's go up Calvary.'

And so we journeyed homeward, Crunch complaining about the hill he'd christened Calvary. He'd wheeze and pant and stop every so often to hold on to walls and railings, piling on the pain. 'Hang on Davy, slow down a bit,' he'd beg. 'I'm not able,' he'd say as I tried to coax him up the hill.

Until we came to The Friary that is - a sad quaint chapel that would be more at home in a Billy the Kid story, somewhere deep in Mexico - and his eyes twinkled with mischief and I knew well enough what he was going to say.

'Let's go in and see The Little Saint,' he said, walking on into the chapel yard ahead of me.

He was forever comparing me to this young martyr whose bones are buried beneath a wax statue of the dead boy inside the chapel. Everyone lovingly refers to him as The Little Saint in the Friary and local legend has it that he was killed by his cruel father who hit him with a hatchet because the boy defied him and received Holy Communion. Crunch said I had the same sort of unfortunate face as The Little Saint and that he could just imagine me '*laid out*' like that in the casket with a great hatchet mark on my forehead.

We entered the chapel and blessed ourselves from the huge holy water font inside the door. A man who didn't look too well was ambling from station to station, genuflecting and praying. There were a few children lighting candles and giggling and some old woman whistling out a rosary in the transept. We tiptoed up a side aisle, our feet clacking on the shining tapestry floor. When we reached the shrine we knelt down at the small altar and I blessed myself again and said a few prayers. As I turned to see if Crunch was ready to go I realised that he was sort of shivering and shaking all over, laughing uncontrollably as it turned out and trying to hold it in. I nudged him to stop it, which of course only made him worse, and he spurted out a loud grunting laugh that escaped down through his nostrils. The woman, who was leaving, turned to see what was going on. The man saying

The Stations Of The Cross did too.

'I can't help it,' Crunch spluttered. 'Every time I see you I think of The Little S ...' and he laughed into his hands.

I got up and walked away from him, pretending to be black out with him. The woman, who was a formidable looking harridan, had actually stopped at the end of the chapel and was glaring blatantly at the pair of us. Crunch was walking behind me now and still laughing. As I passed the woman I heard him snort and I fell victim too. I tried to let on that I had an awful cough, taking out my handkerchief and burying my face into it as I rushed headlong to the door.

Outside, the chapel yard was tinged with a rainy hue. Rain clung to the eaves of the old church, and through the leaves and branches of a sturdy chestnut tree pearly drops fell and rustled in bunches to the ground.

When Crunch came out he was wiping the laughing tears away and saying, 'Do you know what Davy, every time I see you I think of The Little Saint ... I can just imagine ... Hello missus ...'

The woman came out of the chapel and passed us by without answering Crunch's hello.

'I can just imagine you laid out like that and I'm standing over your corpse that way,' Crunch went on and he rehearsed how he would stand over me with a big sorrowful face on him. "Poor Davy," I'll say. "His Da hit him on the forehead with a hatchet because he wouldn't get his hair cut." And your Ma will come up to me and hand me your guitar. "He wanted you to have it, Crunch," she'll say.'

'Yeah and you'll head straight for Ned Stand's and pawn the feckin' thing on me,' I chipped in, and he laughed and mimed the scenario – guitar, money, door!

'How much have we left?' he wondered when we reached the gate and I began counting the remainder of our winnings.

'Well, there's one pound one and six anyway,' I began. 'One pound ten and a tanner, there's another ten bob, that's two pounds and sixpence. And there's a nice little half crown... What does that make it?...Two pounds and three shillings. Two pounds three and thrupence...'

All of a sudden Crunch grew impatient to be off and he told me to cut out the shilly-shallying, give him a few quid and let him go. I handed him the lion's share and before I knew it he was walking away from me, calling over his shoulder that he might see me tonight. He seemed to be heading for Stafford's of John Street. The climate in The Shamrock wouldn't be too pleasant right now- *Tailor's Hall* was well down the field and to make matters worse the horse that beat him, *The Cat's Whiskers*, was ridden by that Jonah of a jockey called Gordon Glynt.

Before Crunch disappeared around the bend he stopped to natter to some old woman in a doorway. 'Go away ye cur,' she shouted after him as he sauntered out of sight.

CHAPTER TWO

The train trundled up the quay, puffing and spouting like a big wounded whale. The Woodenworks creaked beneath its heavy weight and the engine let out a long lonesome moan as it ploughed past the Talbot Garage and the hissing gasworks yard. It clattered roughshod over the coin that had been planted on the tracks by a gang of squabbling schoolboys, their dancing shadows waving and cheering like Red-Indians. The pipe-smoking old men sitting on the seat in The Crescent Quay wisely held on to their words and let it pass. The fishermen, who were lugging big wet sacks of mussels onto the wharf, had to shout to be heard. And then the blue sky turned white as the noisy locomotive rattled by The Shamrock and The Small Hotel and the White Horse Inn to roll through the dismal goods yard and on towards the newly painted North End Station.

Hickey's beery breath fogged up the window as he gazed out onto the platform where people were being greeted, hugged and kissed and carted off to idling motor cars. Well, it was still the same old station anyhow, he had to admit, pulling his black bag down from the rack above his head: the familiar moon-faced clock, the heavy scales in the corner, the cold impersonal waiting room, the handcarts and the lethargic porters who pushed them; he took in the blue pocket of sea in the gap between the buildings too, and the flagged floor and the weather-vaned turret. It struck him that the sight of it all actually hurt him as he stomped out his half-smoked cigarette and alighted.

He was standing beneath the bustling, green-pillared pavilion now, surrounded by passengers who came and went, boarding and disembarking and embracing: that Protestant-looking lady, haggling with the red faced hackney man (she'll get no change there); the sandy haired porter tramping by, busying himself banging doors and yodelling like a town crier, the handover hoop looped around his wrist; a man and his son lifting a wicker pigeon basket from the goods wagon as the regimented station master looked on, flag and silver whistle at the ready.

Hickey was a strong man with a rugged face and slightly hooded eyes and calloused working hands. He was small in height but his body was hefty and he had developed a knack of concealing his drinking paunch. He was known to have a fairly short fuse, although generally speaking by nature he was a quixotic man, confining his blows to gigolos, bullies and smart Alecs.

Today he felt tired though, and defeated, and he could tell without looking that there was a fair amount of pain in his smile. Coming back can do that. A hometown can pare down your accomplishments to the bone, dry them up and blow them away on you. Accomplishments! He was returning home to Wexford no better off than he had been before he'd left it in the first place, sixteen-odd years ago. He had a Sunday suit that was frayed at the edges and glistening with age and in his wallet there was about twenty-five pounds, a ticket to the Galtimore Ballroom and a torn picture of a woman he'd sooner not recall. There was a bellyful of memories too - of cold wet building sites and greasy spoon cafes, miserable boarding houses and reeking Irish bars; there was a fractured nose and a busted thumb and a propped up note in an envelope with his name on it, a discarded wedding ring inside. *Meself and Toby have decided to...blah blah blah...* Rolled up and palmed away, picked up and straightened and read again...*Myself and Toby* if you don't mind!....And shortly after that he had to come back for his poor mother's funeral: the pain of that! And going back to London after his first Christmas home, and every other Christmas afterwards for that matter. And the summer was nearly worse, well just as bad anyway. Although worst of all was the very first trip over. Himself and Farrell, mere garsúns at the time, crying their eyes out on the deck of the mail boat beneath that frosty, starry sky.... *Meself and Toby have decided to* ...what?... No... All smudged.

Hickey pulled himself together, shuddering as the sandy haired porter came his way – *Ladies and Gentlemen, at enormous expense the incredible mind-reading Mickey Morris and his musical hoop!* Hickey faked a smile and trudged towards the gate, his shabby black bag (Doctor Kildare the boys had dubbed him in the Elephant and Castle) scraping against his leg.

Outside, on the wide-open street, he grinned at the sight of Victor giving instructions to some stranger who had lost his bearings, Victor pointing and waving like a wound up toy soldier.

'Your man'll be rambling around half the night,' Hickey said to the sandy haired porter who was coming out the side gate behind him.

'Oh stop,' the porter replied as he slyly slipped across the busy boulevard to The Monument Bar.

Hickey had no real plan. He just walked and his feet automatically took him towards The Shamrock. He had seen it from the train, along with the trail of confetti that led from there into The Small Hotel. Now as he drew nearer he could hear the faint sound of an accordion and see a band of spruced up wedding guests trooping out of The Small Hotel and into The Shamrock for, presumably, a bit of a singsong.

First of all he would book a room for the night. Tomorrow he would look around for a place of his own and try to pick up a bit of work somewhere. He'd been away long enough, he told himself, he was home to stay now. Darkness was creeping over the town as he stepped under the lantern-lit canopy of The Small Hotel. A paperboy's phantom voice howled like a lone wolf a few streets away.

Hickey checked into his room, unpacked his bag and arranged his stuff in the drawers of the dresser - shirts in one, underwear and socks in another. He stripped to the waist and had a quick wash in the sink. He lay down on the bed for half an hour but he was too restless to sleep and so he rose up, put on a fresh shirt and went down to the dining room where he treated himself to a high tea: sausage and bacon and liver, a few lamb cutlets and chips and brown bread and a silver teapot of tea. He went up to the bar afterwards and had two or three pints of Guinness and one or two half ones. A few hours later he staggered out onto the street. It was dark and The Shamrock was basking beneath a cone of lamplight as a plaintive *Danny Boy* came spilling out into the night. Two men were arguing and jabbing threatening fingers at each other. There was a woman in between them and she was trying to encourage them to come back inside. Hickey cocked an ear and, satisfied that nothing would come of it, he went lurching into the bar, giving a light drunken skip as he went.

It was a smoky scene that greeted him. Paddy Wolfe sat on the soft seat, playing his piano accordion, the tiny scut of a cigarette clinging to his sticky lower lip and the long grey ash growing with every pull, threatening to fall any day now. A feeble rebel sing-song had struck up down by the dart board and although it jarred and vied with his own session Paddy, unperturbed, carried on regardless. Young Davy was working behind the counter and never even registered Hickey grinning there beside the snug.

'Hey Wolfe, are you not discovered yet?' Hickey joked as the boy skipped through the crowd with a tray laden with drink.

'Hickey! I never saw you there,' Davy cried. 'When did you get in?'

'Just there now. Well, a few hours ago, like,' Hickey said as he followed the young lad through the red-sea parting of people.

'Hickey, me auld segotia, you're lookin' well, were you sick?' Paddy Wolfe said between lines and without missing a beat. 'Fancy seeing you here,' he added in a posh voice as Hickey took the butt out of his mouth and stamped on it, stuck another cigarette in and lit it up for him.

'There y'are, Paddy, that'll keep you goin' for a while,' Hickey chirped and before he knew it he was down in the corner shaking hands with Johnny and Joe Crofton and giving the sleeping Forty Winks a kind of a hug.

&

My father moved from song to song with ease, feeling it in his bones that there was a whale of a session brewing. He smoked, sang and coughed all at the same time and eventually one by one the drinkers reluctantly joined the caravan.

Though April Showers
May Come Your Way
They Bring The Flowers
That Bloom In May
Cause When It's Raining
Have No Regrets
Because It Isn't Raining Rain
You Know
It's Raining Violets….

Johnny was in position beside him, throwing in odd bits of harmony and scatting like Louis Armstrong. The crowd loved him and obeyed to the letter of the law the instructions that wafted from his invisible baton. Sometimes he let them soar. Other times he took them right down, squeezing all their voices into a tiny space between his hands, giving the whole thing cadence and rhythm. My father liked his style and- to let him know- would wink up at him on and off.

Hickey was playing darts, singing as he fired. Joe Crofton was enjoying the session too. Joe Crofton was a regal sybarite, straight-backed and smirking. He sang out of the corner of his mouth, hoping that somebody else would get the blame. During all of this I was running around like a blue-arsed fly, serving, collecting glasses and wiping tables, and maybe passing out somebody his change at the same time. Forty Winks would come up for air every so often and mutter, '*the name's… Timmy,*' or, '*give the man a chance,*' or some such thing.

When Johnny sang *The Whiffinpoof Song* the entire place fell silent. It told the story of a bunch of misfits who were about to go on a dangerous mission from which they would never return. Johnny looked real moody as he peered out from behind a wreath of swirling smoke, and the way he sang the song made us all feel that we were those men who were about to die.

We Are Poor Little Lambs
Who Have Gone Astray
Ba Ba Ba.
Little Black Sheep
Who Have Lost Our Way
Ba Ba Ba.
Gentlemen Songsters Out On A Spree
Doomed From Here To Eternity
May The Lord Have Mercy
On Such As We
Ba Ba Ba.

During the last chorus Lar Lyons nearly ruined the whole thing by imitating a sheep and he was duly crucified for it, Joe Crofton giving him the evil eye and Forty Winks drowsily cursing him into a knot, so that in the end I'd say Lar Lyons was sorry he spoke at all.

Then Hickey called on my father to recite *The Farting Competition* and, seeing that there were no women present and that it was Hickey's homecoming, he obliged. This was a vulgar recitation that went on for ages with my father taking off all the different accents and facial expressions of the people competing and the clergy who blessed the occasion and so on:

I'll sing you a ditty that's certain to please
Of a contest in farting at Stockton-on-Tees
Where all the best arses paraded the field
To compete for a prize of various shields

This year's competition drew in a large crowd
And the betting was even on Mrs McCloud
For the news had leaked out in the mid-day edition…

I, having heard it all before, was tiptoeing around in the background, finishing off somebody's pint of stout and taking somebody's mimed order and letting someone else know in dumb show that I was on their case.

That this lady's arse was in perfect condition…

The vicar arrived and ascended the stand
And there he addressed the competitive band
"The contest is open as shown on the bills
We've forbidden the use of injections or pills."

Forty Winks, wide awake now, gave him a hand with the last line and grinned broadly when Johnny encouraged him, 'Good man, Timmy.'

Old Mister Jones had a massive backside
With a crest of hair and a wart on each side…

Some of the people who had never heard it before were in stitches and the ones that had heard it before were laughing at them laughing. One fellow nearly had a hernia. He was holding his side with the pain and the tears were rolling down his face. Then to make matters worse a fellow called Durango Clark did actually break wind, rather loudly as it happens, and the whole place exploded. 'Open that window, Davy,' someone shouted and all the doors and windows were dramatically flung open.

In the meantime, needless to say, my father never wavered.

Next on the scene was Mrs McClean
With her cheeks painted red
And her hole painted green.….

By now men were careened against each other, hugging one another and holding each other up. Durango Clark was actually sitting on the floor and another lad – on hearing the verse about the bold Willy Wight – had to go down to the toilet to try and get away from it all. 'Stop,' he was trying to say as he went, waving them all away.

'fo… fu's sa…sto..'

People passing by outside stopped to have a look in at this laughing bar and soon a noticeable crowd had gathered on the street and they were all laughing too even though half of them hadn't a clue what was going on. Victor was there among them with a big idiotic smile on his face and I heard one old man remark as he walked away, 'that must be a great pub altogether.'

When my father eventually finished the recitation he thanked Durango Clark for the special effects and the whole thing, which had more or less died down, started up again. It was time for the grand finale after that so my father picked up the accordion and guided us from *Have You Ever Been Lonely* into *Martha, Carolina Moon* and finally slipped into *Irene Goodnight*. Everybody knew that their time was short in The Shamrock when they heard *Irene Goodnight* and I was inundated with last orders.

'Davy, give us another drink here when you're ready.'

'Yeah, right, Hickey, just one second. Durango, there's your pint. What did you ask me for? A what? Two pints and a glass.... Thanks Durango. Jem says he has enough.'

'Davy did you get me that drink yet?'

'What did you ask me for?'

'I asked you for the same again.'

I'll See You In My Dreams.

The smoke filled pub was a battlefield now with frothy glasses lining the bar and knocked over bottles spitting their dregs onto the floor, which was already littered with squashed fag-ends, scattered confetti and crinkled-up racing dockets *(6d's each way double on Whitfield Lad and…)*. I squeezed past the men in the snug to turn off the outside light and to close over the front door.

'Don't serve any more drink, Davy,' my father said, laying down his accordion for the night and launching into his usual routine of trying to clear the house. 'Right now children, devotions in the morning at the usual hour, followed by a short instruction.'

A dribbling drunk who hadn't uttered a word all night started singing *Carrig River*.

'Oh no,' my father complained, throwing his eyes to heaven. 'I wouldn't mind but he knows all twenty-seven verses.'

> *The Hawthorn And Sweet Briars*
> *They Would Your Heart Illume,*
> *And The Rippling Of The Waters*
> *When The Fraochals Were In Bloom.*

Old Willy crawled from word to word, making heavy weather of it, as my father paraded through the crowd like a policeman, shouting at the top of his voice, 'Come on now gentlemen, have you no homes to go to?'

'Stop the noise, Paddy,' Hickey slurred.

'Are you goin' to drink that pint, Hickey, or make soup out of it or what?' my father said, putting his arm around Hickey's shoulder. 'When are you goin' back anyway?'

'Aw give us a chance, Paddy, I'm only after gettin' here,' Hickey pleaded.

My father grinned and moved along, saying to Johnny as he went, 'You'd better give Rip Van Winkle a shout there,' and Johnny began shaking Forty Winks awake.

> *'Tis Well I Do Remember*
> *When Together We Did Roam,*
> *Through The Lonely Dells Of Carrig*
> *Where The Woodcock Makes His Home.*
> *All Nature It Is Smiling*
> *Upon Each Rocky Side....*

One by one they reluctantly departed, some of them taking wrapped up parcels of drink with them. My father was on point duty at the door, overseeing the exodus and making sure none of them sneaked back in again.

'Are you alright, Johnny? Can you manage?'

'Yeah, game-ball, Paddy,' Johnny said as he helped Forty Winks to his feet and out the door and then he stopped to whisper confidentially, 'The blind leadin' the blind.'

And The Silvery Stream
Flows Down Between
To Join The Slaney Tide.

'Willy, you can give us the second instalment tomorrow,' my father said, leaving his post and coming across to guide the old singer out the door.

'What's it doin' out, Paddy?' Joe Crofton called over his shoulder when the door was shut behind old Willy, who could be heard singing his way up the street.

'It's a grand night,' my father said, sweeping the floor.

Joe Crofton lowered his pint, picked up his coat, which was draped across a high stool, and made for the door.

'Good night, Paddy,' he said and peeped in at me and called, 'good luck Davy.'

'All the best, Joe,' we said in unison and my father sighed to see the last of them go.

When I had most of the glasses washed my father told me to go ahead home, saying that he would finish up, and, being weary of the busy day, I grabbed my 'bum freezer' and went. Joe Crofton was standing outside, buttoning up his overcoat and tucking himself snugly into it. Old Willy was still giving *Carrig River* socks a few doors up while Hickey could be seen slouching in the hotel porchway, ringing the residents' bell.

'A grand night says he,' Joe Crofton chuckled when he saw me there. 'I wouldn't mind but it's freezin' brass friggin' monkeys out here.'

Lar Lyons flagged down a passing car and secured a lift home.

'There he goes- Rigor Mortis Junior,' Joe Crofton said, pointing him out with his head.

The quay was practically deserted except for a boy and a girl kissing in a shop arcade and a perished young guard blowing into his hands. We crossed over onto the Woodenworks to avoid getting tied up with old Willy and I slowed down my pace to suit Joe Crofton's tipsy swagger.

The tide was high and the rain-swollen river was preparing to wage war on the unsuspecting ocean. Behind us the bridge was just a shadowy shape hiccupping to the other side and Useless Island looked close enough to touch. When I said that it was a wonder someone wouldn't build a casino or something out on Useless Island Joe Crofton gave the idea some thought and kind of smiled at my ingenuity. I secretly wondered if he ever felt trapped here. He'd been around, I knew that. He had worked on the buildings in London with Hickey in the early days. I'd often heard him mention The Elephant and Castle and the Edgware Road and all the rest of it. One day, when I had saved enough money, I would break away from here too. I'd take my guitar and go away and come back rich and famous and cock sure of myself. I'd buy up Useless Island and build that casino. *Casino Blue*, I'd call it. Or *The Lady Luck Cafe* maybe.

'Will this casino have a whorehouse?' Joe Crofton inquired out of the blue.

'Yeah. Upstairs,' I assured him as if it was all planned.

Joe Crofton allowed himself another regal smirk as we crossed over into Cinema Lane and very soon the two of us were swallowed up by the darkness.

§

Down the red coloured, carpeted corridors of The Small Hotel an ancient grandfather clock ticked away the seconds, chimed away the hours and let the years slip serenely by.

Beneath bedroom doors tiny beams of light squeezed their way to freedom. Behind one of those doors two illicit lovers lay entwined; and two doors up an away-from-home plumber sat on the side of his tossed bed, stretching and yawning and making strange faces. In Room 22

Hickey smoked his first cigarette of the day while next door but one the worn-out commercial traveller applied a bit of rub and spit to his stained, striped, buttoned down, two-tone shirt.

On this wet spring morning George splashed his way through the front door and wiped his feet thoroughly on the thick rough mat. He brushed off the drops abruptly, shaking himself like a dog in the hall as the rain trickled down his round face and onto his solid heavy-set body. He discarded his drenched overcoat and hung it up to dry in the built-in cubby-hole beneath the stairs. Down below the jangling sound of the kitchen coming alive could be heard and George, satisfied that things were stirring elsewhere in the house, began his busy day. George was the head barman (and the head bottle-washer) in The Small Hotel. He knew exactly what had to be done and he did it. First off, a blazing fire had to be lit in the bar and another in the residents' lounge. It was not technically speaking his job but the young lad would take forever and he would only wind up doing it himself anyway. After that he might do a bit of stocktaking in the bar before nipping out to the new Cash And Carry on The Redmond Road. As George disappeared down the stairs to the yard the sleepy-eyed bell-boy with uncombed hair and a pimply face shuffled into the dining room to turn on the radio, set the tables, polish shoes and call the early risers.

Mr Martin lived in the back of The Small Hotel. Unlike the rest of the guests he stayed there permanently. He got a special rate: a clean room, breakfast, dinner and a light tea. All found, seven pounds, seven and six. He rose every morning at eight-thirty, although he woke up much earlier than that. He washed, shaved, dressed and carefully trimmed his moustache, which he quaintly referred to as his *ronnie*. On weekdays he wore his light blue three-piece suit, his white blue-striped shirt with a change of collar each day. Sundays were special. He got up at half seven and went up as far as eight o'clock mass. He wore his best suit on Sundays and a sparkling white starched shirt and his brown Winstanley shoes.

Apart from these he did not have all that many clothes really. He did not believe in hoarding. There were a few sports coats and summer things: these were neatly folded and packed in the lower drawer of his dresser. God only knows why he ever bothered to keep them. Summer was so short nowadays that it was harmless. Why, he could remember when he was a boy - May to September and the sun splitting the trees! It was all these rockets, he was sure of it.

Mr Martin was banking on not living more than another five or six years at most. He did in fact pray for it. In five years, according to his own reckoning, his savings would have dwindled considerably and he would no longer be able to live like this, he would be forced to lower his standards and he asked God to spare him the embarrassment.

His day usually followed a delightful pattern that he had lovingly designed: Ten o'clock Mass in the Friary, a morning newspaper, a brandy and port in the snug of The Shamrock public house, a bet on a horse, a short nap, dinner at one, a glass of porter in the front bar of The Small Hotel, a stroll along the Quay (this of course depended on the weather) and perhaps a chat with some of the other old timers who normally sat on the wooden seat in The Crescent. And then, money permitting, another glass of porter in The Shamrock. After tea he watched the box in the television lounge, which was his right and privilege. But apart from 'The News' and a few other topical programmes he found most of it out-and-out drivel. He usually retired to bed early with a good book. He loved Steinbeck, Dickens and Hemingway and some of the great Irish writers. He found Joyce offensive. We were all well aware of the human weaknesses without being told all the time. He liked thrillers too and, even though he said so himself, he was uncannily good at detecting the culprit. He completely disregarded books and authors that stooped to sex and violence. He was well over seventy now and never in his long life felt the absolute need for either one of them.

True, he had not accumulated a lot of worldly possessions in his lifetime. He looked across at them now as they stood side by side on his dressing table: a good pipe, the likes of which you would not find today; a gold watch and chain with the phrase **Per Semper Idem** engraved on the back of it, given to him by his comrades and associates in the Civil Service, which seemed to imply that he was well thought of and genuinely liked. This surprised him at the time for he had never gone out of his way to make himself likeable. On the other hand he had never deliberately set out to annoy or infuriate anybody either. No, he spoke his mind and begged to differ. People did not always like that. Placed between the pipe and the watch was a sepia toned, framed photograph of his mother and father on their wedding day; and close at hand, lying face down for some reason, was another snapshot of himself and his brother, Ernest, in short sleeved shirts by the seaside.

Had he not been so offhand with people he just might have married - a plump country girl with spectacles and a kind smile. Now the only thing he had to remember her by was the after-effects of a hug that had lingered all these years and a dainty novelty cigarette lighter she had given him one Christmas Day. Or was it Stephen's Day? Whatever! He picked it up and rolled it around in a warm cupped palm. Then he held it up to the light just to see once again the slender ballerina who was immured in the see-through casing. With the slightest provocation the dancer twirled and pirouetted and sort of curtseyed. He allowed the ghost of an ironic smile to surface: the dancer was everything his poor plump country girl could never be.

When Mr Martin descended the creaking staircase George knew that the day had well and truly begun. The old man stopped as usual to synchronise his watch with the grandfather clock on the first landing. The big boy was the boss. If a BBC announcer said the time was three minutes to nine and the big clock said it was not, then the BBC was wrong.

Mr Martin greeted graciously the rugged looking joker from number 44 who was going down the stairs in front of him. He had seen him someplace before but could not recall where or when it was exactly. He shook it aside and carried on down into the white linened dining-room where he commandeered a table comfortably close to a luke-warm radiator. He picked up his napkin and draped it across his lap. Then he blessed himself and, as he cut into his grapefruit, he secretly thought, 'What a way to die!'

&

'Listen Davy,' my father said as he climbed into his top-coat, 'Johnny Sligo is in town.'

'Is he? Who was tellin' you this?' I chirped, delighted with the news.

'Never mind that,' my father said. 'If he comes in here don't serve him any drink.'

'Why not?'

'Because I don't want that jowlster hangin' around here, that's why,' he snapped, heading for the door.

Johnny Sligo was a street singer, the last of a dying breed, and I was disappointed that I would not get to hear him play. My father never elaborated on people's characters: you were either a '*jowlster*' or you were not.

Crunch was down in the corner, nursing an unmerciful hangover and Rocky, my little terrier, was tormenting him, snooping about and getting under his feet.

'Crunch, you keep an eye on things while I'm gone,' my father said before he went.

'What? Yeah right, Paddy, leave it to me,' Crunch vowed and wearily covered his head in his hands.

Johnny Sligo, as I forgot to mention, was six feet tall and built like a battleship. If he did come through the door it would have to be crouched and sideways. Needless to say I grew a tad nervous as I watched my protector fidget and silently plead with Rocky, who was barking at a cat that was perched outside on The Small Hotel glass-topped wall.

My father had only coughed his way around the corner when the sun-lit doorway was eclipsed by a big black shadow. It was what you might call a magic doorway. From behind the counter you could see into the future - wives after unfaithful husbands, fathers after their blackguard sons, unwelcome drunks who would, given half a chance, slobber and slouch all over everyone. The frosted glass afforded you a vision of sorts, a vague premonition you could say of what lay ahead. Not long enough for you to make any alternate arrangements mind you. No, just a slight hint of what the immediate future held in store. So I closed my eyes and cursed as Crunch peeped out from behind his spread out fingers.

Johnny Sligo tarried on the doorstep and tried to place the bar. He'd grown a beard since the last time I'd seen him and his hair was longer. He was surrounded by instruments - a guitar dangled from his neck, a hurdy-gurdy, tied with twine, was hanging around his back, and in a makeshift case he carried a banjo, while a rake of tin whistles sprouted from his pockets. He stepped inside, grinning at Crunch and bending down to pat Rocky's ears.

'How's it goin'?' Crunch said as Johnny Sligo stood up from his hunkers and approached the counter.

'Not too bad,' Johnny Sligo said. 'How is yourself?'

Crunch just shrugged, suspecting (spurred by my distraught face in the mirror no doubt) that he'd already overstepped the mark.

Johnny Sligo divested himself of his instruments and lay them down against the soft seat. 'Give us a pint of cider there, son,' he said then and I glanced across at Crunch for comfort.

Crunch winked at me and blurted, 'Here, I'll pay for that drink, Davy,' emptying his pockets noisily out onto the counter.

'Nice one,' I snarled as I scooped up the money: he didn't even have enough to pay for it.

'Davy, that man would put the pair of us in his pocket,' Crunch said. 'Anyway, won't you hear some good music.'

'Huh,' I grunted, thinking that it might be my last session when my father got a hold of me.

Soon the word got round that Johnny Sligo was in The Shamrock and in dribs and drabs people started coming in. He drank two pints of cider before he sang at all. He was sitting over on the soft seat and tuning up his instruments. Eventually when he considered it worth his while he began to play, coming over and plonking himself up on a high stool close to the counter.

Barelegged Joe knows the curlew's cry.
He can run like a hare through the soft, green corn.
He can sing like a lark in the early morn,
On the bright green hills of Sligo.

I was trying to watch his fingers as he played, keeping an eye out for any interesting chords or runs that he might use.

'Where's that pint, Davy?'

'What? Oh, I have one on for you.'

'You've got a drink on for me too, Davy!'

'Have I? Oh, right!'

'Lord Jaysus, ain't that awful. I asked him for a drink about a half an hour ago. You'd want to wake up there.'

I served them in a hurry for fear I'd miss something. George came in and closed the door of the snug behind him. I spied the white coat through the corner of my eye and turned to see what he wanted. He motioned *'the usual'* which was a small bottle of stout. I opened one for him, slipped him an empty glass, and let him pour it out himself. He looked at me askance when he saw Johnny Sligo, knowing full well how my father felt about buskers and then he lowered his drink and left.

Meanwhile Johnny Sligo was in full flight. He sang sea shanties like *Sally Brown* and thumping war songs like *Kelly The Boy From Killane,* and tender love ballads like *Matt Hyland.* He told stories and yarns that took us to foreign lands or transported us across the country in a tinker's barrel topped wagon. We slept beneath the frozen stars, and woke in the morning, the grass wringing with dew. He sang of emigration - *Paddy's Green Shamrock Shore*- and recited bits of poetry too.

I do not grudge them: Lord, I do not grudge
My two strong sons that I have seen go out
To break their strength and die, they and a few
In bloody protest for a glorious thing.

And then he ploughed straight into *The Foggy Dew,* strumming furiously on the banjo.

'That's a right stave now,' a fat man said, and gave me the bend for another drink.

'I'll be shot,' a fellow in overalls mused, and glanced fleetingly at his watch. 'I only popped in for a quick one.'

'Aw sure what's your hurry,' the fat man belched. 'You'll be dead long enough. Davy, give this man a drink here too.'

'No, I've to go. Honest to God.'

'Go on out of that. Have a pint. Sure it won't kill you or anything. Give him a drink and don't mind him.'

'I'll have a glass, Davy.'

'Give him the pint. Sure you might as well be hung for a sheep as a lamb.'

'What about yourself? Do you want a pint or a half one?'

'What? Give me the two of them. A bird never flew on one wing. Ain't that right?'

'What's that?'

'I say a bird never flew on one wing. Ain't that right?'

'That's right.'

'He did not. Give the singer a jar as well while you're at it... Jaysus, don't leave out the band anyway or there'll be war altogether. *And The Angelus Bell O'er The Liffey Swell/ Rang Out Through The Foggy Dew.*'

'I had a dog once, lads, and this is no lie,' Johnny Sligo began. 'He was so cute he could play the bones of Carolan's Concerto on the concertina. And he could ride a two-wheeler bicycle provided there was no bar on it. His name was Weasel but he would only answer to the name of Bonzo because the Law was after him....That dog could whistle *The Boys of Wexford* better than any man here and he could make a fair fist at yodelling *Lovesick Blues*. Then I discovered that he could walk across water. No, that's a fact. I was as surprised as you are now. I threw a stick out and told him to fetch it and off he went walking across the water, picked up the stick and brought it back to me. I couldn't believe my eyes. So I tried him again and sure enough off he went across the top of the water. Mind you, it was cold enough that day. The next day was fine and sunny however and so I tried him again and when he performed in much the same manner... I shot him.'

'Shot him,' the fat man said, alarmed. 'Are you out of your... A dog like that was worth a small fortune, man.'

'You must be jesting, sham,' Johnny Sligo retorted. 'Sure that dog couldn't even swim, boy,' and, snare snapped, he launched into a jig which he announced as *The Cat Shat In The Coal Hole And The Monkey Slapped His Arse.*'

My favourite was *Bogie's Bonny Belle,* an old English folksong, and for this one he used the strange-sounding, droning hurdy-gurdy. I was miles away, listening to him, and there must have been a broad smile across my face because Crunch leaned over at one stage and said, 'I don't know what you're looking so happy about. Wait till your da catches you, he'll give you the greatest box in the forehead you ever got.'

'And you,' I reminded him.

'Oh, not at all. I was not of sound mind and body when I volunteered for that job,' Crunch pointed out, and then informed me with his head that George was waiting to be served.

George indicated *'the usual'* and mumbled, 'Christmas already,' as I gave him his change.

Two posh-looking women, who had come in earlier on, called for two more dry sherries and told me to give George a drink too, leading me to presume that the pair of them must be staying inside in The Small Hotel.

George flinched at being detected. 'I'll have it later on, Davy,' he said and he drank up and hurried back to work.

One of the women, the petite one, asked Johnny Sligo did he know *The Lonely Woods of Upton* by any chance.

'What's that?' Johnny Sligo said, turning to face her.

'"*The Lonely Woods of Upton*",' she said, and she demonstrated.

> *Many hearts were filled with anguish and with sorrow*
> *Many homes were filled with la la la la lay.*
> *La la la la la la la la la la la,*
> *To the lonely woods of Upton far away....*

The Lonely Woods Of Upton? Do I know them? I often slept in them,' Johnny Sligo joked.

I couldn't help thinking that if a more robust lady had asked that same question and twittered so badly Johnny Sligo would have used a different euphemism for what he got up to in the lonely woods of Upton.

Lar Lyons picked up a deep ashtray and went around the bar, taking up a collection for Johnny Sligo (trust him to get in on the act). Crunch, who didn't have a button, tried to ignore him but Lar Lyons stood beside him for ages, shaking the ashtray and grinning like a moron. Slowly Crunch turned and bared his teeth until Lar Lyons finally got the message and moved along.

Johnny Sligo asked me to turn all the small change collected into notes and told me to give Lar Lyons a drink. Lar Lyons protested, faking a great surprised expression and saying that he never expected a drink. In a flash Johnny Sligo was gone, sparing me a farewell glance before he went.

Crunch assumed command then and he called across at the two women, guessing where they came from.

'Aw, you're miles out, boy,' the big one said.

'You're not a Cork woman?' Crunch chanced, dubiously.

'No,' the big one said, emphatically.

'I'd say you had some connection with Cork then,' Crunch ventured, and the woman smiled wryly to insinuate that he had hit a nerve.

'I married a Cork man,' she admitted as Crunch inched his way towards her.

'Don't mind me askin' you, but what's your name,' Crunch said, and when she looked up at him indignantly he explained, 'I've seen you somewhere before. I was just sayin' to young Davy there,' (which he hadn't) '"I know that woman," says I. Excuse me for intruding but what's your -'

'O'Shea,' she said.

'O'Shea. What's your husband's first name?'

'Eddie.'

'Eddie O'Shea. Was he a seaman?'

'No,' she said and the sadness in her voice, and the way the petite one dropped her head beside her, indicated that the man was recently deceased.

'Eddie O'Shea,' Crunch kept repeating over and over again as if he was trying to put a face to him.

I went about my business, washing glasses and filling up the empty shelves, secretly thinking that Crunch was barking up the wrong tree there. But fair play to him when I turned around to serve George the bottle of stout he was owed there was the bold Crunch sitting on the soft seat between the two women, bamboozling the pair of them with stories of the sea.

'Give these girls a drink,' Crunch called, banking on them refusing, which of course they did.

George, from the safety of the snug, shook his head and dryly said, 'Huh, girls is right, one of them has so many wrinkles I had to give her a hand to screw her hat on this morning.'

The girls, both of them, bought Crunch a drink: two large bottles that before the night was out would become a bottle of whisky, and before the end of the week would have grown into an afternoon's drinking and a fiver into the top pocket, and maybe some sexual intrigue too into the bargain.

'Crunch is in his alley,' I said to George as I watched him mould out Indio for them - her neck, her shoulders, her breasts, her big legs.

'A jowlster, if ever there was one,' George said and he vanished, planting his frothy glass on the narrow ledge in the snug before he fled.

CHAPTER THREE

Rowdy Row looks down on the sea from above. If you slip down the grassy bank and scramble across the railway line you'll find what they call the Shelter, where the ocean is surrounded by a shingled shore. Here the oil skinned fishermen work, mending their nets and caulking their flat-bottomed boats. Look up and you'll see a shambling stretch of curtained windows where toothless widows gab and shuffle slipshod from house to house, where gangs of crop-headed urchins gatch and play amidst a shantytown of slung up sheds and lofts and shabby dog boxes.

It is a gable-end house. The garden is weedy and overgrown with bits and pieces of prams and wheels strewn all about, and there is the ashy scar of a burnt-out bonfire. Lean hungry looking children huddle together on the front step. The window has a pane missing and the door is paint-scraped and tatty. Inside there is an untidy margarine kitchen and a coughing wheezing woman. And there is Dancer - her bane-eyed, vindictive husband. The commotion in next door's backyard tells him that all his neighbour's birds have been mauled to death. God help all tomcats tonight. Dancer milks pleasure from it, his face aflame.

'All the same, he was dyin' about them pigeons,' she says.

'Fuck him. He never did nothin' for me,' Dancer spits with a glassy-eyed glance.

Dancer didn't have a pigeon loft. He had no dog, no cat, no boat, no apple of his eye, no nothin', and he had to laugh at all the lovers and losers and hopeless dreamers he spied as he staggered up Rowdy Row late at night. He had a high forehead and prominent cheekbones and the way he dressed would have been comical on anyone else - the buttoned-up tie-less shirt, the wide shapeless pants and the loud coat belonging to some other suit. But you could look at Dancer forever and not find anything to laugh at. There was nothing funny about him: not the scut of a fag that was eternally wedged behind his ear, not the dirt between his fingernails, not the bawdy songs he warbled all over Easy Going Larry late at night, not even his snoring when he was flaked out on the sofa in front of the fire in the middle of the afternoon.

Dancer had no time for the traditions and superstitions of Rowdy Row. On one occasion they say he borrowed a boat and sailed out of the harbour on Saint Martin's Eve, a day and night when no real Wexford fishermen would dare put out to sea. He was gone all day and as the sun dwindled a small group of people lined the stony strand, concerned for his safety. The man who owned the boat paced up and down like an expectant father, feeling kind of responsible and already mourning the loss of his boat and gear. And then a speck appeared on the horizon and the murmuring crowd, somewhat embarrassed by it all now, began to disperse. Soon Dancer tied up the boat in The Shelter and he had a fine catch of herring in the hold. He offered half his haul to the owner of the boat but the man refused to take it, saying no good would come of it. 'Suit yourself,' Dancer said, and it was later reported that he was sneering as he scrambled up the ferny bank.

&

We came out of the dingy hotel ballroom and waited beneath the winking neon sign. Inside a brutal dance band was massacring *Take These Chains From My Heart* and from where I stood I could see the tubby bouncer hitching up his pants and admiring himself in the glass doorway. Across the street a radio blared from a parked car and Lar Lyons, who was passing, stooped to study its occupants. We were waiting for two girls who, thanks to Danny's coaxing, had agreed to let us walk them home. This was quite a coup for us. This dance hall was a kip and talent was usually scarce on the ground. Our real dancing season would not begin until next month, when all through the summer season the Parish Hall would be packed with lovely girls and the best bands (The Freshmen, The Greenbeats and the Miami Showband with the soulful Fran O'Toole). Meanwhile this would have to do us, and to pull two girls from here was an unusual occurrence to say the least. Furthermore, if these two Rowdy Row women lived up to their reputations, then Danny and I would be doing the light fandango all the way home tonight.

When the door squeaked ajar both of us stood erect and turned to see Rocky, my little white terrier, coming out. Danny's face dropped and he went back to leaning against the wall again. A few seconds later the bouncer was out and hunting the dog away from the entrance. Rocky had followed me in, sneaking past the doormen, and all night long he had shadowed me around the hall, even when I was dancing with someone. Once or twice I'd lose track of him only to spy him a few minutes later up on a chair, scanning the hall for a sight of me. Then he'd eye me, wag his little butt of a tail and, delighted, come clicking across the powdered dance floor.

'Do any of you own that dog, lads?' the bouncer wondered.

'No,' I said, sensing that he had been up to some mischief.

The bouncer picked up a stone and flung it after Rocky, who went hightailing it out of there.

'Why, what did he do, Bruiser?' Danny asked.

'The little fucker is after pissin' all over me,' Bruiser complained, and shook his leg. 'I was just standing in the hallway there and up your man comes as nice as you please, cocks the leg and psst ....' and he went back inside with a vexed face on him.

'He'll be gettin' us killed,' Danny reckoned as Rocky skulked back up the street to join us. 'Here we go.'

The two girls were in the porch, laughing at the bouncer who was telling them about the dog pissing all over his leg. We were standing in the shadows like two hard-chaws when they came out.

'God, you frightened the life out of me,' my one said as we pounced: I think she must have forgotten about us.

A few minutes later we were up behind the gasworks yard wall and Danny was claiming it as his territory. So I headed for the deserted railway station and we ended up inside the falling-down waiting room. In the darkness she filled up my arms and ran her fingers through my hair. Her kisses were passionate and tinged with desperation, but when I tried to put my hand up her jumper she stopped me.

'No,' she said. 'Don't.'

'No?' I said.

'No. Just...you know...Hold me or something...' she said and she sort of snuggled into me, her head on my chest.

I just let her lie there awhile. I could smell her lacquered hair and her cheap scent and the stale taste of cigarettes whenever she said something, and I made up my mind not to try again. I also decided I wouldn't tell Danny about it. He'd only say, 'What did you stop for? They all say that. That doesn't mean you should stop. They have to say that.'

And of course that was all very well but... well, if she didn't want it then I didn't want it either and that all seemed fair enough to me. All of a sudden the place lost all sense of romance and when she commented on the rotten smell I realised the jig was up. I followed her out onto the platform and she called out, 'Annette, I'm goin' now.'

'Aw, wait a minute,' a voice came back from the darkness.

I was standing on the deserted station, trying to act like a hoodlum, but feeling a bit of a heel. Rocky, who was sniffing around in the weeds, heard the voices and came galloping towards us. When the two girls were reunited they linked one another and, once I was given a passionate farewell kiss (from both of them), they disappeared - like two unlikely angels - out of our lives for good.

Danny came out of the shadows with his shirt hanging out and went behind an old battered up goods wagon to have a leak. I sat down on the stone platform with my feet dangling over the edge as Rocky inspected the disused waiting room. Danny would later confess to me that he got nothing either. She put her cold hand inside his shirt and tickled his back and that was about the extent of it.

Across the way the squealing pig factory was silent and the lofty signal box seemed to creak for no real reason. In the dark the station looked like a tumbledown gazebo, windswept and overgrown with nettles and weeds; all of this combined with the salty tang from the sea triggered a recurrent childhood memory that is both vivid and painful for me. Suddenly I'm a boy again and all my summers are crammed into the one day, sometimes the one moment. I'm on a train heading for a day trip to the beach. We stop at this very station and it's a hive of activity - women yapping, men smoking, tough looking gurriers running riot. This place reeks of the sea. The people do too, and the train. They cram on board, pushing and shoving like it's the last train to paradise. They clamber into our carriage to crowd up the aisles and sit on the tables and swing from the overhead racks. Wherever there's room they squeeze in and they have no manners and they seem to have all the answers. This is the other side of town (and the other side of the world for that matter) as far as I'm concerned, and I'm intrigued by their withered faces and their perpetually harangued expressions and their wily ways. Who are all these people? Where do they live? Up there somewhere, is it? And there's a child there all on his own. Who's supposed to be minding him? How had he reached up to buy his ticket in the first place? How will he know when we are at the beach? I'm pressed up against the window. My mother is sitting opposite me with my baby sister on her lap. These boys look tougher than anyone on our street. I bet they can run faster, spit further and hit harder than any of us. The boy beside me says bold words. I feel kind of timid now and sorry in a way that we've come at all. In a way I'd prefer to be back in our tiny house in John Street, playing with my toy soldiers. My mother seems to sense my fear. She asks me if I'm alright. I tell her I'm grand. My mother prays all the time. She prays to the Little Flower, St Theresa of the Roses, but it never seems to do any good. When I got my hand caught in the spokes of the bicycle that time and lost the top clean off my finger she cradled me in her arms and tried to hush away the pain as she paced the floor with me. There was a trail of blood leading out through the front door and across the street and a troop of wide-eyed children standing in our doorway as my mother kept repeating over and over the little prayer she used to say:

Little Flower
At This Hour
Show Us Your Power
For The Love Of Jesus.

And later when she walked down those hospital steps without me I couldn't help thinking that the Little Flower mustn't have heard her.

The train is chugging out into the countryside now, leaving behind on the platform a boy and girl holding hands. They must have changed their minds I suppose. All around me voices gabble:

"Here me little gentleman", says I to him, "I want a word with you."

"Eamon get down out of there. You'll fall. That's a cur.... Here's the man."

"Hey Marie, do you want to sit on my lap, hon?"

"Get out of it ye dirty divil."

All of a sudden I'm afraid and I don't know why. Maybe it's these familiar-looking strangers and the way they carry on. No, there's something else. What is it? My mother hasn't paid for me, that's it. She's trying to sneak me down for nothing, as half the mothers on board are doing. If the ticket collector asks me I'm to say . . . I wish we didn't have to do this kind of thing. My mother brushes back my hair from my eyes and smiles. She says I must have been a little prince in another lifetime.

'Hey Davy, do you want to go up to Peter Dempsey's for a feed or what?' Danny yelled, emerging from the darkness and stuffing his shirt back inside his pants like some satisfied Latin lover.

⁂

Mr Martin tucked his galoshes and raincoat neatly and definitely under his bed and then crossed the floor to open up his window a fraction. He frowned at the din from the street below which filtered in to fill up his tiny room. He was dressed in a sports coat, a flimsy sleeveless geansaí and an open necked summer shirt. These, of course, had been properly aired before he ever even dreamt of wearing them. He had asked the boy to put them in the warm cupboard on the landing.

Looking down on the thriving street he recalled how only the other night he had heard Matty McGuire's voice as he escorted a band of tourists through the town. Matty was an out and out genius on the history of Wexford and its surroundings. Nothing could fluster Matty. Not even the cheeky corner-boys who were shouting unrepeatable remarks and slogans at the visitors. Matty, who was a gentleman, just ignored them and trooped on by, pointing out something of interest as he went and maybe answering someone else's question at the same time.

It was only then when the smiling troop had gone on by that it dawned on Mr Martin that it was actually the summer. Lord bless us and save us tonight, it had never even occurred to him. For all he knew this could be the last summer he'd ever see. Well, he would celebrate it as if it was his last. Yes, tonight he would dig out his summer clothes and tomorrow he would ramble out into the bumbling countryside to breathe in God's own fresh air. Apart from the clothes and the walks in the country his schedule would not alter all that much. He might from time to time drink a pint of ale shandy instead of his usual glass of porter, which was a bit on the heavy side for this time of year. But other than that things should remain more or less the same.

And so when he came into The Shamrock that afternoon I didn't notice any great change in him. There was a bit more gaiety in his stride perhaps and a little more colour in his cheeks, but it was the same old Mr Martin who plonked himself down in the snug and said, 'A pint of ale shandy if you please and go easy on the lemonade.' Then he curtly informed me, sparked off by my Beatle boots no doubt, that the Beatles were a crowd of long haired eejits who were hell bent on leading the younger generation into a barbaric way of life. Manners, morals and respect, he said, were a thing of the past and before long common decency would go out the window with them.

I let him ramble on, having heard it all before. I was miles away anyway. Danny had been in earlier on to let me know that there was a barbecue on out in Ferrybank that night. He said that it was being organised by a crowd of girls who had just finished their exams and that by this time tomorrow the pair of us could be bar mitzvah material. He said that Skeleton Delaney, who was Danny's sexual mentor, had assured him that this barbecue was the place to be tonight.

'How could you call that music,' Mr Martin was saying. 'I mean noise, that's all it is. There's neither sense nor meaning to it,' and he was away on a tirade about the Beatles, or the Beagles as he called them. 'No sense to it,' he said. 'Yeah yeah yeah...'

Girls, girls, girls. Big ones, small ones, ones as big as your head and me and Danny in the midst of them. Maybe Linda might be there with her poodle. Rocky could handle that. He loved poodles. He got one in trouble one day up on our street and they had to rush her off to be doctored. They would have doctored Rocky too if they had been able to catch him.

'Do that fella ever shut up?' the unshaven character with the pencil behind his ear said, loud enough to stop Mr Martin mid-sentence. There was a long embarrassing silence then which ended when Mr Martin finished his drink and left with a great haughty goodbye as if it was all my fault. They laughed of course, delighted that they had driven him out.

'Hey Davy, how is your da goin' to survive if he takes his business elsewhere?' the unshaven character with the pencil behind his ear sneered.

'Yeah, a pint of ale shandy and he thinks he owns the place,' Lar Lyons commented, cute enough not to say anything while the man was there.

'Who does he think he is anyway? Lordin' it up in the snug. Is he too good to come out here with the rest of us or somethin'?'

'I don't mind tellin' you but he has nothin' to be uppity about then,' Lar Lyons said and off he went - seed, breed and generation.

I picked up Mr Martin's glass and began washing it over and over again, blocking out their stupid voices and drifting off into the future. Linda was down on the beach waiting for me. I ran towards her and she caught my hand and led me up into an out-of-the-way place behind the bushes. She lay down of her own accord and smiled up at me invitingly. My little heart was thumping inside my shirt as I approached her.... Wait a minute. I'm supposed to work tonight. Shite, I forgot all about that... I'll have to ask my mother to stand in for me... Yeah, I'll ask her. Now, where was I? Oh yeah, Linda was lying down of her own accord and I was approaching her with my little heart thumping inside my shirt. Hang on. Go right back to the beginning again. How did you shift her in the first place? How did I shift her? She remembered me from that day Crunch and I were in The Hole In The Wall. It was my smile she remembered. She said she didn't know who I was at first, that she knew she had seen me somewhere before. But it was when she saw me smile that it all came back to her. She said I had a deadly smile and I started up this little game with her, with me smiling all the time, and she ran away from me, glancing over her shoulder to see if I was following behind her, but I had circled round her you see and I was now directly in front of her. She thought that was cute and she put her arms around me and kissed me. And that's how we ended up in the bushes with her lying down of her own accord and me approaching with my little heart thumping inside my shirt.

'Give us another large bottle there, Davy.' It was the unshaven character with the pencil behind his ear again.

I told Linda not to budge, that I would be back in a few shakes of a dog's tail. I pulled the large bottle, took his money and gave him the wrong change.

'Hey Davy, it's dear enough,' he exclaimed.

'What? How much did I?... Oh!'

'His Da has him well trained alright,' Lar Lyons snickered.

I rectified the matter and hurried back to the sink where Linda should be still waiting for me, but unfortunately their stupid voices had frightened her away.

'I don't like talkin' about anybody,' Lar Lyons was saying, 'but I know for a fact that he came from a family that hadn't a bean to their name. He was born and reared in a falling down cottage no bigger than this place here and there was a dose of them in it too. I'd safely say in his younger days he saw more dinner times than dinners now, the same fella.'

'And where did his nibs get his notions from then?'

'Now that's the hundred dollar question...' Lar Lyons said and away he went again.

I felt a twinge of rage seeping through me. I mean I didn't agree with everything Mr Martin said or did or stood for but I had to admire the way he stood apart from the rest of them. This crowd of begrudging bastards wanted everyone to be tarred with the one brush. Don't go getting any fancy ideas of your own whatever you do. Dance like everybody else and don't go inventing your own steps.

I mean Joe Crofton didn't take offence from Mr Martin's manner. In fact I think he was fairly fond of him. I remember one Christmas Eve Joe Crofton sent Mr Martin in a brandy and port and wished him a Merry Christmas and in return he received a polite wave and a slightly confused smile. And Johnny always doffed his hat, so to speak, to the old man. And Crunch never uttered a word - good, bad or indifferent - about him, which I suppose was a sign in his favour.

No, it was only Lar Lyons and the likes of him who took offence. They probably talked about us too - the family I mean. If they wanted to they could go back to the time we lived in that scutty house in John Street. We were a poor family then with our Da working away in England and our ma praying all the time to The Little Flower.

I can still see that dark living room where she used to work. I picture her wiping her hands, white with flour, and she coming across to fix my hair, saying, 'All the girls will be after you now, Davy boy.' The mantelpiece laden down with stuff: the clock with its secret hiding place in the back, the Sacred Heart Lamp, the rent book, the insurance book, Father Gaul's penny bank card to see us over the Christmas, the steel comb that was always supposed to be hidden out of sight, and the crackling old radio dishing out *Take Your Pick* and *Mrs Dale's Diary*. The tattered horse-hair sofa which became a mountain or an ocean or a desert for me and Mickey Fury who lived with his granny a few doors up. And my mother would often toss Mickey Fury's head of hair as if she already knew what was in store for him. And on wintry nights we'd all sit around the blazing fire and my mother would read us the letters from England. We'd toast bread skewered on a fork and my mother's soft lilting voice would weave out a little Shangri-la of words for us just to ease the awful lonely pain of growing up.

'What did he work at anyway,' the unshaven character with the pencil behind his ear inquired between gulps.

'I don't know…The Civil Service I think,' Lar Lyons said

'Davy?'

'What?'

'Where did your man work before he…The Civil Service was it?'

'What?'

'He's away in cloud cuckoo land there.'

I was too. I was trying to remember what Mickey Fury looked like. We were inseparable in those days, reading each other's minds, fighting one another's battles. Mickey was there when I got my hand caught in the spokes of the bike and he tried to hug away the fright and the pain. But I broke away from him and he followed the trail of blood that led to my house and he stood in the hall and watched my mother cradle me in her arms. And Mickey saved my life once. I was drowning and he awkwardly splashed out to get me, risking his own life for me. I never got a chance to repay him. He ran away to sea when he was sixteen and I never saw him again. He handed me a letter that I was to give to his granny when he was long gone. Then he shook my hand like a man and he disappeared down a back street away from me. He'd been talking about going for ages but I never thought for a minute that he would go through with it. Late that night I slipped the letter under his granny's door and bolted. I waited at home for her to send for me and to tell you the truth I hadn't a clue what I was going to say to the woman. Like I've said, I never saw Mickey Fury again. His ship went down off the coast of Galatz. It was bound for Newcastle with a cargo of coal. All hands were lost.

'Davy, was it the Civil Service or the bank aul' Martin worked in?'

'Yeah.'

'Which?'

'The Civil-fucking-Service,' I said.

I should never have let him go.

Skeleton Delaney was a genuine juvenile delinquent with all the usual bad habits: he was a shark at snooker, a dapper at cards and according to himself he was the biggest stud this side of Enniscorthy. He could pull cigarettes out of nowhere and what he didn't know about horses and jockeys and trainers wasn't worth mentioning. He could spit like a punk and, although he wasn't much older than any of us, wisecracks and smart remarks tripped out of him with all the confidence and flair of a married man.

Now as I played the jukebox in Nolan's Cafe, Skeleton Delaney was giving Danny a lesson in how to play table football. He was assuring Danny that this barbecue would be absolutely crawling with talent tonight - nymphomaniacs, willing virgins, the lot. No, he wasn't going out there himself. He had a few other things to take care of he said as he banged in the last goal, giving Danny what was known as '*the brush.*' Then he picked up his lighted cigarette from the ashtray and with a great cocky swagger he was gone out the door.

Danny bought himself a coke and moseyed in to where I was standing. We moved to a table and took stock. It turned out we had the price of a few pints between us by my reckoning and maybe one or two beers to take out to the barbecue afterwards.

We decided to go down to The Small Hotel and as we passed The Shamrock I peeked in through the tiny window to see my mother scurrying around inside. I couldn't make out my father but we could hear his vamping accordion accompanying Johnny, who was singing *Heart of My Heart* and as we slipped into The Small Hotel they changed key and shifted artfully into *Have You Ever Been Lonely.*

'It's well for some,' George said as he poured us two pints of ale.

A commercial traveller called him over and asked him, 'Where did

I see that chap before?'

'That's Paddy Wolfe's young lad,' George told him. 'Next door,' and the man sent us across two more pints with his compliments.

'Cheers,' I said, holding my brimming glass aloft.

'Keep them coming,' Danny murmured under his breath.

A few hours later Danny and I were walking across The Woodenworks and the music from The Shamrock was just a faint tinkle in the background. The sound of an Irish tenor floated out of The White Horse Inn as we stepped onto the bridge where a man and his son softly cast their fishing lines into the phosphorescent water below. A purple tint enveloped the harbour and the sun, slyly slinking down behind the gasworks, was doing its best to set the sky on fire. We joined the clinking procession of young people who were trudging across to the other side of the river. When we arrived at Ferrybank, the crowd, which had more or less snowballed together on the way out, began to splinter, some of them scattering off up into the Dairy Fields. We stuck to the strand, a mangy stony excuse of a beach where only the most ardent swimmers swam. The Dairy Fields (better known to us as The Babby Factory) we'd prefer to save for some glorious moment in the future when some strange passionate girl would lure us up into the long grass. Then from out of nowhere Rocky materialized, wagging his bare butt of a tail and barking.

'Where did he come from?' Danny trumpeted.

'I don't know,' I said and clapped my hands, which was a sign for Rocky to jump up into my arms like a circus dog. 'Good boy Rocky baby,' I was saying, scratching his ears as he licked my face. 'He's the smartest little boogie woogie baby in the entire world.' I was going on like this and putting on a ridiculous voice when a few gorgeous girls who were passing caught me at it and laughed. Danny walked on ahead as if he wasn't with me. I felt obliged to keep going until they were out of sight. 'He's a wikkle washal so he wis,' I was saying, and Danny was up front, sitting on a sandy bank and shaking his head in mute condemnation.

A couple, in deep conversation, were going the opposite way to the rest of us. She was telling him all about her blessed exams which she had just finished and that she hadn't done a blessed thing all year and that she didn't think for one blessed minute that she was going to pass the blessed thing. Everything was blessed except Sister Anita, who was an out-and-out bitch in her heart.

'Hey, any pass outs?' I asked them as they went by and Danny forgave me and grinned as he recalled all the nights we had to stand - stone broke - outside the dancehall: we'd wait and hope that someone would click with a girl and come out early so we could pounce on their pass outs and get into the dance for nothing.

Danny threw a stick out into the sea and told Rocky to fetch it. But Rocky was having none of it and cocked his leg instead.

'That's a lazy fucker, that fella is,' Danny said, laughing at the idea, and I waded in with a few lines from the recitation *Life Gets Tedious Don't It*. (It has to be done in a cowboy accent).

> *The hound dog howls he's so forlorn*
> *That's the laziest dog that ever was born*
> *He's howlin' 'cause he's sittin' on a thorn*
> *And he's too darn lazy to move over.*

Danny joined in on the last line with me and he clapped his hands for Rocky to jump up into his arms like a circus dog, but Rocky wouldn't do that for anyone else but me.

Then a big fellow - let's call him Longfellow for the sake of it - called down from above:

'Hey you two'.

'Us little old two,' I called back, still in my cowboy accent.

'Where's this barbecue?' Longfellow bellowed abruptly, a big country head on him.

I reeled round to Danny and said, 'No please or thank you or anything.' Then I turned back again and proceeded to dole out directions:

'Turn around,' I said. 'Well you don't have to turn around if you don't want to but unless you're able to walk backwards I'd say you should turn around. However, it's entirely up to you. Anyway turn around or don't turn around and go out through that gap there and straight on for about three or four or maybe ten miles or whatever until you come to a gate. Open the gate or jump over it, depending how agile you are by then, and you'll find yourself out on the road again. I'd suggest you start thumbing then and try to get to the nearest town, where maybe you could book into a hotel for the night ... .'

Longfellow was already walking away by now, saying, 'Very fucking funny.' But I was still giving him the instructions, shouting after him.

'In the morning, if you have any money, I suggest you catch a train to Belfast. From there you'll have to get a boat that will take you to the **Virgin Islands**.... 'I was shouting at the top of my voice and Danny was breaking his heart laughing and saying that I was drunk, which I suppose I must have been.

We walked a few hundred yards and decided to take a rest on an old fallen tree. We opened two beers and Danny skipped his bottle top across the water. I smacked a drink and belched and said to Danny, 'Here, skip that for me there,' and Danny took this invisible thing and kicked it off up the bank.

Darkness had crept over the town and a firmament of lights winked across the bay, mapping the skyline. On the other side a goods train shunted through the dishevelled depot, its beating heart hissing and pulsing in the distance. Somewhere over our shoulders there was the lure of distant voices and crackling fires and giggling girls. We listened and dawdled on that old fallen tree for a while, drinking, belching and singing and Rocky roving. Time enough!

We arrived at the barbecue to find two fires going, one small one where they were dishing out food, and a large one, around which everybody sat and sang. Somebody had a guitar and they were singing *Mister Tambourine Man*. Linda from The Hole In The Wall was there. She was standing on top of a hill, talking to this rugby-type bloke, touching his scarf.

'A scarf in the middle of the summer,' I scoffed to Danny as he branched off.

I went across and got some food, a few burnt sausages on a stick and a plastic cup of oxtail soup. As I sat on the grass and blew my soup cool I heard somebody scream, 'Who owns that fucking dog?' Rocky had grabbed a dose of sausages and he was running around growling and shaking the string like a dead rat between his teeth. He ran off into the bushes with a few annoyed cooks throwing sticks and stones after him. 'Kick the shit out of him,' I shouted and couldn't help thinking: fair play to you Rocky, boy, at least one of us made it into the bushes.

Danny was across the way chatting up some pretty girl. It turned out to be the girlfriend of the big fellow who had asked us for directions. Longfellow came back and glared at Danny, who just proceeded to sing along with the music as he casually danced away to safety. Behind me there was a girl who was holding her mouth and wincing with pain.

'What's wrong with you?' I said to her. She didn't answer me. 'You haven't been poisoned or anything like that I hope, have you?' I joked, sniffing at my soup.

'No, toothache,' she then said and rocked herself gently to and fro.

'Ouch,' I said in sympathy, rolling over onto my belly, closer to her. 'I suppose you just finished your blessed exams as well, yeah?' I said, supporting myself on my elbow and gazing up into her face.

'What? Oh no, that's Alice. You've tried her too, have you?'

'Alice. Aw no, we're just friends,' I lied.

'She invited you, did she?'

'What? Yeah, that's right. Me and Danny.'

'Who's Danny?'

'You know Danny,' I said, and pointed him out with my head.

'Oh, Danny Newman. You're not Davy Wolfe by any chance?'

'Yeah… How did you know?'

'Danny Newman and Davy Wolfe. It's like Laurel and Hardy. Mutt and Jeff,' she said and stood up. 'Danny Newman and Davy Wolfe,' she said, sort of shrugged and left.

'Well, I'm gettin' rid of him,' I called after her. 'I'm goin' solo,' I said.

She went across and asked some girls if they had anything for pain and lo and behold one or two of them actually did, rooting in their bags and rummaging in their pockets and what-have-you. I followed her with my eyes as she went to lend a hand doling out the food. Then Danny crept up to me and told me that he had something important to show me. I told him that we were through, that I was branching out on my own.

'Come on,' he said and led the way.

We traipsed out into the darkness and then at his signal we dropped onto our stomachs and crawled up a bank and peeped down the other side. First off I couldn't see a thing, but when my eyes grew accustomed to the night I spied two bodies in swimming. They were naked and when they came out of the water I recognised them. They were a young couple who had been going out together for about a year and a half now. Everybody knew they were mad about one another. They kissed standing up, their naked bodies gently touching.

Then as if obeying some invisible signal the pair of them lay down and snuggled into one another. Another fellow was lying beside us now, a freckly faced cross-eyed looking lad who just appeared, unannounced, out of nowhere. Soon the young couple were making love, actually doing it right in front of our very eyes. We could see them move, hear them sighing out their sweet nothings. But, I hasten to add, we weren't the voyeurs we intended to be. No, we were three wise men sent to witness the conception of a little red headed boy that would be born nine months from now. He would grow up and never realise that Danny Newman and Davy Wolfe, the Mutt and Jeff of Wexford, had actually witnessed his beautiful beginnings. When they had finished doing it they just lay there, him on top of her, and the little cooing sounds they made were soft and sexy. Eventually there seemed to be an unspoken general consensus that we leave them in peace and so we crawled back the way we came, and as our little trio approached the sparking fires all three of us agreed that she was a grand bit of stuff.

&

Kathy, the one with the toothache, walked on ahead of me, backwards so that she could hear what I was saying. She looked as delicate as anything walking there beside the sea. I was showing off, skipping stones across the top of the water for her. When she tried to do it she failed miserably. I demonstrated, exaggerating the earnest, distorted look that was on her face when she threw. I overdid her stance as well so that in the end I looked like a dowdy old woman who was awkwardly trying to throw a javelin. I accidentally toppled over onto the ground and incorporated the fall into the act too. She turned her back demurely saying, 'Well, I never,' as she went.

'No, Kathy, watch. I'll show you with ... maybe you couldn't see properly when I was using such... tiny stones,' I said and I lifted up a gigantic rock and ran to her side.

'What?' She turned and laughed as I tossed it out into the water. It landed with a splash, spattering the pair of us, her more than me since I was using her body to shield myself. She gasped and I put my arms around her and drew her closer to me. Then she smiled her little gap-toothed smile and we kissed for the first time, a harmless peck.

'Look at my sister's jeans with you,' she mourned.

'You'll get your death. You'd better take them off,' I joked. 'I'll light a fire and we'll...'

'Get out of it,' she laughed and broke away from me.

Just then Rocky arrived on the scene, gasping and panting and black out with me for going home without him. Kathy looked like she had just seen an apparition.

'That's the little rascal who stole all our sausages,' she cried.

'That's the same lad alright,' I said and clapped my hands for Rocky to jump up into my arms like a circus dog, but he wouldn't.

'Is he yours?' she asked.

'No,' I said. 'I'm his. Ain't I Rocky?... He's not talkin' to me now.'

'Here Rocky,' Kathy said, stooping down, but Rocky wasn't bothered with her at all and went off prowling around, cocking his leg and sniffing out the cockle shells.

The tide was in so much that in places it actually touched the sandy cliffs that climbed up into the Dairy Fields: most of the time we only had a few inches of strand to walk on. Once or twice I had to give Kathy a piggyback, laying down a makeshift bridge of stones first and then gingerly stepping across them. She had rolled her jeans up to her knees and I was carrying her shoes in my hands.

Across the river Wexford sleepily squinted back at us, its dark empty streets echoing with the frightened bark of a locked-out dog and Rowe Street chapel chiming three. Then from a cluster of trees above in the Dairy Fields a wild vixen let out an unmerciful screech, scaring the living daylights out of all three of us. Rocky stopped in his tracks, pricking up his ears. Kathy cried out, 'Jesus, Mary and Joseph!' I got a fright too but I hid it by putting on a devilish leer and limping towards Kathy like a werewolf. She hugged me back to normality and then when she saw me smiling she bravely kissed me on the lips of her own volition.

All the while we talked about our lives and about our future plans. I would break away from here one day, I told her. I'd take my guitar and sing my way around the world.

'What about me?' she pleaded.

'You can come with me,' I told her and kissed her again.

We were kissing all the time now. Every second word was punctuated with a kiss it seemed and I'd wrap my arms around her like a cloak. Kathy said that she wasn't so sure if she wanted to leave home or not. She said that she had worked away all last summer and found it terrible lonely. She painted a picture for me of a small town girl running back to the hostel every night and lying awake in her bed listening to the lonesome sound of the city. She said that even worse than that was when you'd catch a glimpse in at some family kitchen and see them all gathered around the table, laughing or even arguing. She said somehow you don't expect to happen on someone living a normal life in the middle of the city. She had green eyes and a cluster of freckles around the bridge of her nose and as I already said she had a cute, gap-toothed smile.

She asked me if I had some hero that I admired. I said no. I was going to say maybe Mickey Fury who ran away to sea when he was sixteen and went down with his ship 'The Irish Rambler' off the coast of Galatz. But Mickey was a friend not a hero. I couldn't say Crunch. He was not a hero. No. The nearest thing to a hero I ever met was a boy who was in my class at school. He was nothing to look at or anything. I mean he wasn't big and strong or good at sports or anything like that, but he was brave. When the teacher got browned off teaching he would sometimes let us meander out loud about some of the things that bothered or amused us. He might ask us what our fathers worked at and every one of us, including me, would gloss over whatever it was our fathers did. Of course the doctor's sons and the solicitor's boys didn't have to do any glossing, but the rest of us had to, seeing how it was practically a sin to be hard up in those days. When my little hero was asked about his father he said he didn't know. He told us, and the teacher for that matter, that his da had shagged off on them when he was three years old and they never heard tell of him since. That was exactly how he told it too, and nobody knew what to say, not even the teacher.

And another time we were asked what we wanted to be when we grew up. Some said doctors, some said teachers. Others said that they would like to be tradesmen – carpenters or plumbers and the like. When my little hero was asked what he intended to be he said that he'd like to be a diver. At that time the new bridge was being built over the river and there was a lot of talk about the Dutch divers who had come over to work on the project. Most of the lads said that he was stupid. That bridge would last a lifetime and there would be no real call for divers in this town and so he would have to go away to find work and stay away forever more. He just shrugged off their remarks, indicating that he had been asked a question and had answered it honestly. Regarding going away and staying away he said, 'Sure what's wrong with that?'

'What was his name?' Kathy wondered.

'Anthony Taylor,' I told her. 'He's probably in some mental home as we speak somewhere, suffering from the bends or something… Oh, blub blub blub blub…'

We were on the bridge now. Below us the River Slaney had joined together all its gushing streams and angry rivers, all its ponds, brooks and reservoirs and was rushing on to join forces with the sea. The Shamrock was in darkness and from where I stood I could just make out the last bedroom light flicker and die in The Small Hotel.

CHAPTER FOUR

Crunch delved into a torn crusty pocket and retrieved from it the stump of a pencil, a thrupenny bit, a betting slip with a sure thing that - thanks to Gordon Glynt - turned out to be down the field, a few fluffy unused matches, a screw of some kind or another, and finally, from somewhere deep inside the lining, the bare bones of a Woodbine cigarette.

Main Street was awash with visitors these days: jaded, receding men in short-sleeved shirts and their refined wives who issued forth orders in put-on English accents. Victor was there too, dressed in a bizarre Hawaiian shirt, supervising the summer season.

I know that man, Crunch was thinking as he lit up. Paddy Whats-his-name. He left here a pauper and returned fairly prosperous. A marvellous country altogether! Oh, Nancy, you've a grand arse for a lazy…. 'Hello Toddy, what way are you?'

'Hello there. How are you keeping?'

'Not too bad, and yourself?'

'Oh, can't complain, can't complain.'

Crunch carried on. 'He don't know me at all. No, he don't. Sure it must be ten or fifteen years since I last saw that man. More, I'd say. It was the night Hickey's old mate Farrell knocked him out. Dead as a cock. And I had a pound note on the winner. I bought him a drink and everything afterwards when he came to. Little did he know.'

Easy Going Larry was loitering at the foot of Keyser's Lane. Crunch became conscious of him there but he hadn't time to alter his course now. Easy Going Larry put on the poor mouth and Crunch threw his hands up in despair. Easy Going Larry eyed the cigarette sorrowfully. Crunch sighed, admired the fagend, extracted one last passionate drag and handed it over. Easy Going Larry took it discreetly, his eyes flickering about in a cloak-and-dagger fashion. Crunch took out the betting slip and squinted at it.

'Did Dixie Dandy win?' he wondered.

Easy Going Larry gave it the thumbs down. Crunch was well aware of that already, he just wanted Easy Going Larry to know that he wasn't holding out on him. Now he crinkled the docket up into a tight ball, cursed Gordon Glynt into a knot, palmed it away from him and went. Behind him Easy Going Larry had waylaid some other poor unfortunate and, chances are, money was changing hands.

The Bull Ring smacked of a Parisian square with the sun sweltering down on it in splashes and the tiny shops winking at the droves of people that passed to and fro and back and forward all day long. Behind the iron market-gates Tom Furlong's butcher shop bustled and the flower sellers and street traders called out their wares. Cheap Charlie, the most famous and charismatic of all Irish street traders, cried through a megaphone:

'Step up this way ladies and gentlemen. Come on, I won't bite. I can't anymore. I haven't any teeth left. As Our Lord said to Peter, "Peter come forth," and poor Peter came fifth and lost the blooming race. And the Lord also said, "Thou shalt not steal," but you have my permission to ignore that one today because at these prices you're robbing me blind and that's all's about it. You should be ashamed of yourselves. Do you see these lighters here, a lady's and a gent's, both of them suitable for cigarette smoking and pipe smoking and cigar smoking and, if you like, chain smoking. Up the town you'll pay a fiver for the pair of these. Ladies and gentlemen, at the risk of being committed, I'll let you have the pair for three quid. No, listen I'll tell you what I'll do and I must be after going soft in the head altogether, but I'll let you have the two of them for thirty

bob. Ah, to hell with it, here take them and be done with it for one pound
note and the first one to purchase will receive an autographed copy of
my latest record which is available from any respectable police barracks
around the country. Yes and we have a buyer: sold to the man with the
new hat. And there you go, sir. Just look at that pound note smile. It
hasn't seen the light of day for over seventy years or more. Wasn't that
Queen Victoria a bad looking woman all the same, sir....? '

Crunch sat down on the plinth of the Pike Man monument and
drifted into a melancholy daze. Johnny's Shoebox was spic and span
and open for business. Johnny was there in his dainty apron as he
wrapped up a pair of recently mended shoes (soled and heeled and
a new pair of laces) in an old newspaper, licking his thumbs and
grinning and singing a snatch of a song. And Ned Stand was sitting
outside in the shade and calling to the boy who was working inside
the cluttered-up pawn office; the boy was hanging up a battered old
pram with a long pole (like a fishing rod) and asking Mr Stand, 'How
much is this worth, Boss?' In between these two shops Joe Shiggins,
the sour-faced barber, had his place. The Last of the Mohicans was
his nickname and Crunch spied him scalping some unsuspecting
youthful-looking farmer. Svelte young girls went rushing by, ignoring
the wolf whistles of the sturdy messenger boys. And there was Victor
again, standing under the chemist's clock like a garda, and Mr Martin
from The Small Hotel dandering up Cornmarket.

Crunch hated this time of year, everyone acting so efficient all of
a sudden. Even The Shamrock had acquired a business-like manner
with Davy running around the place like a maniac, talking and counting and muttering; and Paddy greeting perfect strangers as if he had
known them all his life, and he was as hoarse as a crow from all the
singing. Nobody had time to talk anymore. What's more, and worse
again in his book, nobody had time to listen.

Johnny stepped out into the sun for a few minutes. He stretched and
yawned and called across to Ned Stand. The railwayman gee-upped
his dray horse into a weary canter and they left behind a fast running
river of urine that flowed all the way down to the Quay, spreading out
to form a myriad of tiny rivulets so that Crunch was marooned in a

sort of a delta. And it was there in The Bull Ring with Cheap Charlie preaching in the background and Wexford bustling all around him that Crunch decided what must be done: he would go back to sea.

♪

Hickey dressed quietly, pulling on his rustling clothes and fastening his shoelaces with an animal stealth. Every so often he would glance across at the sleeping woman who was sprawled out in the tossed bed, and he'd eye her gurgling child in the carrycot.

A shaft of attenuated light streamed in through the tiny window of the beach house as he tiptoed over to the sink to quench his thirst. He put his head down to the tap and glugged a mouthful of water. He could hear the nearby ocean crashing against the shore. He was in Rosslare Strand, a small seaside village which lay ten miles or so from Wexford town. He would have to hitch a lift into work. He'd be late now more than likely and docked a half an hour's pay, but what could he do about it?

Hickey went over and helped himself to one of her cigarettes. He thought seriously about waking her up to say goodbye, but where was the point? He had not climbed to the height of ecstasy last night. He did not experience *de ja vu* when they kissed. He was a man and she was a woman and that was about the size of it, and there was no point in letting on it was otherwise. No, she had not succeeded in thawing him out, with her '*oohs*' and her '*ahs*' and her '*baby baby*'. **Me and Toby have decided to**...Yes, **decided to! Me and Toby!**

He studied himself in the mirror and listened to that far-off inner voice reminding him yet again that there was much to be thankful for - Johnny, for one, who had tipped him off about the room for rent above Ned Stand's pawnshop; and Joe Crofton, who had put in a good word for him with the foreman on the site where he worked; and what about Paddy Wolfe, who loaned him a fair few quid until he got on his feet again? And then there was this woman who had taken a great shine to him.

But Hickey was having none of it. No. The room was a kip for

71

a start and the job was no doddle either, and he'd pay Paddy Wolfe back the money he got in next to no time. And on top of that, while there was something about her, the woman in the bed was no raving beauty or anything. And she had a kid for God's sake! I mean...come on...*Me and Toby have decided to*...or was it *Me and Toby decided to*...Should have kept that note. Ironed it out, flattened it, kept it, or saved it or something. But no, in the bin, in a ball, on the floor. All smudged, all what-do-you-call-it.... And the ring, on display in Ned Stand's pawnshop now, all shined up and shining, shy and ashamed of itself in the window.

'*Me and Toby and Toby and me,*' Hickey uttered like a mantra and the far-off voice fell silent as he picked up his coat and left, the door squeaking gently behind him.

Mary woke up as his feet crunched down the gravelled path. She sat up in bed and caught a glimpse of him disappearing round the bend in the road. She wondered if she would ever see him again. In a way she was glad that he was gone.

&

Crunch was right. We didn't seem to have much time to spare anymore. We were busy '*making the most of it*' and our regular customers suffered because of it (or at least their schedule did). Every fortnight one crowd would leave and another batch would arrive. They were mainly returned exiles, living all year long for this fortnight when they could come back home and see my father perform. He would meet, welcome and woo every single one of them. Every day now he had three stints - one in the morning as hangovers began to fade, a matinee in the afternoon for the mellow punter, and of course the big one at night when the place would erupt into a boisterous singsong.

'Your da keeps us going, Davy,' someone said to me one time and there were tears in her eyes when she said it, and then she turned to her sad faced husband who silently confirmed all the things she said with a dabbed out cigarette.

Of course Mr Martin wasn't over the moon about all this. Often he would jostle into the privacy of the snug only to be manhandled by some singing sailor who would slap his back and bellow, 'Cheer up me old son. Sure you'll be dead long enough.'

'Your father is a great old trooper,' Mr Martin confessed to me one day, raising his voice over the racket, 'of that there can be no doubt, but I do personally find the singing of songs in broad daylight a bit on the vulgar side.'

On another occasion he informed me that it infuriated him to find this mob storming into his life, expecting everything and everybody to just down tools and allow themselves to be whisked along with the tide. He indicated that he had a standard that he had set for himself, a quality of life that was rich and regular, and he had no intention of dancing cheek-to-cheek with every drunken fly boy who passed his way. These fellows, he said, who spent the entire year working and slaving in a foreign country to come back here for two or three weeks and pretend that for them extravagance is the norm. He let me know in no uncertain terms that if I couldn't guarantee him a safe passage into the snug then he would take his custom elsewhere until the heat died down. And that's more or less what he did in the end, what he had to do.

Johnny was off the beer and working hard, trying to get through the mountain of shoes that had built up, courtesy of his last drinking binge. He worked late into the night. Prowling cops would peek into the tiny lit-up Shoebox to make sure that everything was alright. They would see Johnny inside, tapping and gluing and mending and listening to the radio. To avoid temptation on his way home every night he took the back ways. After a hasty slap-up meal he would go to bed early with a good cowboy book and read until he fell asleep. Joe Crofton missed him. He told my father that Johnny had read so many cowboy books over the last month that he was after going bandy.

Eventually Johnny relented. He came out of the shop one night and as he locked the door he heard the music from The Shamrock calling like a distant siren song over the tops of the houses. He went to investigate: he'd have one ale shandy and then go ahead home. Johnny went on a binge that lasted for fourteen days and when it was over he was miles behind in his work and twenty-two pounds in debt.

Poor George suffered most of all. He would come in looking absolutely fagged out and find the snug occupied and the crowd two or three deep at the bar. He would slither in as quietly as he could, trying to look as inconspicuous as possible (which was fairly hard seeing as how he always wore his white hotel coat). He would indicate *'the usual'* and have the exact money ready for me so there would be no, as he put it, *'foostering.'* But some eejit was bound to pass some comment, usually Lar Lyons or the unshaven character with the pencil behind his ear. 'Here's the dentist,' they'd say or, 'Look out lads, The Small Hotel must be on fire,' and George would squirm, gulp down his bottle of stout and mutter, 'Bloody jowlsters,' as he sped.

Late at night when the bar was cleared and cleaned up George would tap on the window and one of us would let him in. He would take down an upturned stool and plonk his weary bones down in a corner somewhere out of harm's way. He'd sit there drinking in silence until my father had finished counting the money and then the pair of them would sympathise with one another and encourage each other on towards another busy day.

⁊

Danny Newman and I (the Mutt and Jeff of Wexford town) walked out of Nolan's Cafe just as The Small Faces' *All or Nothing* came blaring out of the big-winged jukebox.

'Hang on a minute, Danny,' I urged, pausing in the doorway to listen to the soulful voice of Steve Marriot while Danny bummed a cigarette from Skeleton Delaney, who was perched like a villain against a pole outside the door.

Things Could Work Out /Just Like I Want Them To .... I had a good mind to go back into the café again where I could savour the full force of the record - the jangling guitar, the swirling organ, the pounding drums, the pumping bass. *If I Could Have/The Other Half Of You...* An old couple passing by looked at each other and cringed. *All Or Nothing...* Clearly I was not the only one who was affected by

74

the record. There were fellows screaming loudly and other lads banging out the beat on the football table and even Danny (who wasn't particularly musical) was beating the back off Skeleton Delaney. *ALL OR NOTHING...*

'Hey boy, mind the material,' Skeleton Delaney warned him, brushing Danny's hand aside.

When a gaggle of tourists, who were on a walking tour of the town, trooped past, the place erupted, with everyone calling after them, 'Hey, Cromwell pissed here,' and things of that nature. Mrs Nolan had to tell a few lads to mind their language or they would be put out altogether.

We left Nolan's Café to the sound of *Summer In The City* on the jukebox and Skeleton Delaney was wrapped around the pole outside, spitting through his teeth into the gutter.

'Hey Newman,' he cried, 'that's two you owe me,' and Danny tipped him a foxy wink as we walked away.

We sidestepped the crowd of tourists and scooted down Cinema Lane to the Quay where we found a congregation of old men sitting on the wooden seat in The Crescent, Mr Martin amongst them. They were passing round his novelty cigarette lighter, the one with the ballerina on it, and each man had a different technique of examining it. Some of them held it up to the light, squinting up their ancient eyes for a better look, others rolled it around in their speckled hands as if it embarrassed them to have to talk about something so dainty and delicate. Everyone seemed to agree that it was a grand looking yoke, and Mr Martin looked chuffed.

The Woodenworks was bustling with life - families out walking, gangs of teenagers sitting like disciples on and around the bollards, girls in summer dresses promenading and stripped-off messenger boys diving off the broken down derricks - as Wexford tangled and twisted and jumbled itself into a town and tumbled upside down into the sea.

'Hey, there's that little Casey one,' Danny said excitedly.

'What little Casey one?' I said, scanning the street.

'Don't look now. Over there on the other side... Christ, I told you not to look,' Danny scolded me and turned his back.

'How am I supposed to see her if I don't look,' I pleaded, but Danny was vexed at me for looking when I shouldn't have looked. 'What about her anyway?'

Danny made an exasperated sound: he had a good mind not to tell me at all now.

'She's nice, ain't she?' I gushed.

Danny turned to watch her tender distant movements too. 'She is, ain't she,' he agreed. 'Do you know what Skeleton Delaney was tellin' me?' he said and he blurted out all the lowdown on her.

'She went off with Skeleton Delaney?' I said, finding it hard to believe.

'He said she made him swear on his mother's life that he wouldn't tell anybody and as soon as he did he said she hopped off him, boy.'

'Skeleton Delaney, Christ Almighty!' I said, shaking my head and watching her disappear up a side street. 'Did he say anything else?'

'Well he didn't like to elaborate too much he said for fear his mother would drop down dead on him,' Danny continued. 'But he did tell me this though…' and Danny divulged the rest of the hair-raising story.

We were going to a dance in The Parish Hall that night, all dolled up in our mod suits and ties. I was meeting Kathy outside the hall at ten o'clock. Until then we would just lark about and have a bit of harmless sport.

There was a great session pouring out of The Shamrock as we passed. All the doors and windows were flung open so we could see inside. The place was packed and I felt a bit guilty when I caught a glimpse of my poor mother up to her ears in there. George came out of The Small Hotel, stood beneath the canopy and took a furtive look up and down the street. Then he made a dart for The Shamrock, frowning at the crowd of people that clogged up the entrance and elbowing his way through the throng. 'Here's the dentist,' someone said.

We carried on until we happened on Crunch coming out of Roman Lane. He was carrying a bag and he was dressed up like a man who was going somewhere. He saw us and crossed over onto The Woodenworks, stopping in the middle of the road to let a car pass, urging it on irritably with a swish of his arm.

'Where are you off to?' I asked him as he approached.

'Swansea,' he said. 'Give us a fag, Danny'

Danny took a last desperate drag and handed over the scut. Crunch looked guilty as he considered taking the young lad's last cigarette, forgave himself, took it and signalled his thanks.

'What's the story?' I said.

'I'm supposed to join a ship there tomorrow night,' he said, avoiding my eyes.

Crunch had not sailed for years. His kidneys and liver were ruined from drinking. On his own admission the doctor would need to be some kind of dimwit or on-the-take to give him the all-clear.

'El Cruncho strikes again,' Danny was saying and Crunch, who appeared a little downhearted at first, perked up a bit. 'I can just see you Crunch and you knockin' back the vino, surrounded by a rake of big women,' Danny continued.

'Yeah, and I that way,' Crunch agreed, tilting back his body as if he was drinking from a tequila jar.

'Where will you go, Crunch? Will you head down to Valparaiso or what?' Danny probed.

'What? I don't know….I might… You'd never know!' Crunch put his bag down and began fixing his attire, straightening his tie and adjusting his coat collar. 'How do I look?'

'Alright,' I assured him.

'No, do I look OK, though?' he said seriously.

'Yeah, you're grand.'

He shrugged, gave the remark some thought and silently admitted that he would do. Then he said, 'I'll tell ye one thing lads, if ever I do get down around Valparaiso you'll never see Captain Crunch again. I'll stay there. I'll stay with Indio. I should never have left her in the first place. I don't know why I ever bothered comin' back to this kip of a town for anyway. I'll tell you lads and this is straight up, I could have been a made man out there. I could have been King Rat, boy. She had her own bar and everything out there, you know, her own… hacienda. All I had to do was just sit back and let the money roll in.'

'What did you come back for anyway?' Danny asked, trying to

cajole him on.

Crunch thought about it and finally confessed, 'Because I wanted to see Useless Island one more time,' he said.

'Yeah well if you ever do get down around there again and you find yourself in need of a couple of gringos don't forget your aul' mates,' I said just to send him on his way.

Crunch gave a little hoarse laugh. 'A couple of gringos ... ha ha .... Listen I've to go. Thanks for the fag, Danny,' and he reached out and shook Danny's hand. Then he tossed my curly hair, picked up his bag and started to walk away, turning to say, 'The two of you stay out of mischief while I'm gone, because if I get word that you got into any kind of trouble I'll come home and kick the shit out of the pair of you,' and with that he skipped into the old goods yard which was a well worn short cut to the station.

Shortly after that it turned fairly cool and we went up into the shelter of Main Street, turning our backs on the train that was scudding out of town.

&

A few days later he was back.

'He's back,' Johnny declared.

'Who's back?' Joe Crofton said, looking up from the spread-out newspaper.

'Captain Crunch,' Johnny replied. 'I was just delivering a pair of shoes to old Mister Martin inside there and spotted Crunch at the counter. He was a fairly sorry sight to see too, I can tell you.'

Joe Crofton gave a brief dismissive jerk with his head and went back to his newspaper.

'Who is he with?' I wondered.

'He's with your man, whats-his-name ... Dancer,' Johnny said and sort of winced.

'Is George in there?' I said, knowing full well that Dancer was barred from The Small Hotel. He was involved in a big fight one time at a wedding reception that was held in there. They nearly wrecked the place and George said that Dancer was the worst of all, that his behaviour and language was scandalous, and in front of women and children too.

'No, he's not. He must be gone to his dinner,' Johnny informed me. 'The young lad served them. I'd say George'll run the pair of them out of it as soon as he gets back.'

'Well I hope Crunch don't bring your man in here,' I pined.

'Your da barred him, didn't he? Lar Lyons pitched in.

'Yeah, he went to hit Mr Martin here one night and me da threw him out.'

'Ah well, he probably won't come in then,' Johnny reassured me.

'I wouldn't bank on that,' the unshaven character with the pencil behind his ear said, 'knowing Dancer anyway.'

'Sure what harm if he does,' Johnny calmly said, and ordered a pint of ale shandy.

'Here Davy, I'll pay for that,' Joe Crofton offered and he gave me the bend to pour him another drink while I was at it.

Half my mind was on Crunch, who I knew would be down in the dumps now. The other half was on Dancer, who gave me the heebie-jeebies to say the least. I remembered the night he had to be thrown out of The Shamrock, the time he went to hit Mr Martin. My father ordered him to leave and Dancer got up against him, saying that the place was only a fucking kip and that there wasn't a man in the pub who would be able to put him out. Well, he was in the wrong shop for that kind of talk because there were plenty of fellows who would be well able for him. There was my father for a start, who had boxed professionally when he was a younger man; and there was Hickey, who had stood up at the very first sign of trouble. And there was Joe Crofton, who was handy enough when it came to a bit of rough-and-tumble. Anyway, everybody was prepared to leave it between the two of them - my father and Dancer that is - until this Dancer character cracked the top off a bottle and began slicing the air with it. This, along with kicking and head-butting, was considered a ter-rible dirty trick and the whole might of The Shamrock came down on him. He was hit from every angle - Hickey hit him a box in the jaw,

Joe Crofton punched him in the stomach, my father sent a few grand combinations into his face and Durango Clark pushed him into the side of the counter. My mother, God help her, threw whatever it was she had in her hand, which turned out to be a rare china jug, and I ran out through the snug to deliver a fairly ineffectual blow from behind. He was surrounded by fellows in the end, all dying to get a smack in at him, and he ended up outside on the pavement, bruised and bleeding. The last we saw of him he was sloping off up the street and cursing the whole lot of us over his shoulder.

When everybody calmed down, which took some time (some of the lads wanted to go after him and shut his mouth for good), we all went back inside and everybody agreed that he was an out-and-out blackguard and a dangerous boyo to boot. Somebody from Rowdy Row said that it was a known fact that he beat his wife black and blue and that he gave his family a dog's life. The unshaven character with the pencil behind his ear said that Dancer was the only fisherman from Rowdy Row to put out on Martin's Eve. Somebody else objected to this and said that Dancer was not a fisherman at all, that he had no boat of his own or nets or anything and that no real Wexford fisherman would dream of sailing on St Martin's Eve, which was deemed to be a terrible unlucky day.

The bar looked a right mess with overturned chairs and spilt drinks and broken glass all over the place. Everyone gave a hand to clean it up as I poured my mother a drop of brandy to steady her nerves. She was trembling as she drank and mourning the broken jug and my father tried to gloss over the incident saying, 'Sure, no real harm done.'

Mr Martin, who had sat through the whole episode without even flinching, said as he was leaving, 'Sure what can you expect from a pig only a grunt.'

There was some more talk about Dancer, with someone saying that only a cur would go to hit an old man anyway, and when George came in for a quick one he stood and remarked on the serious faces of everybody.

That all happened a few months back and now here was I hoping that Crunch wouldn't land him in on top of me and start the whole thing up again.

'Dancer is a bad herb,' the unshaven character with the pencil behind his ear was saying.

You should know, I was thinking, as I pulled Mr Martin, who had honoured us with a visit, a medium of stout.

'I believe your old mate is inside,' I said to Mr Martin just for a joke.

He knew straight away who I was talking about. 'What? He's no friend of mine,' he objected, paid me, and with a set of wriggling fingers he sent me packing.

When Crunch did eventually arrive into The Shamrock it was hours later and he was alone. He stumbled into the snug and shut the door behind him. His face looked grey and drawn, his clothes were in disarray and he was badly in need of a shave. He called for a whisky and fired whatever change he had up onto the shelf, some of it falling to the ground. He was unable to bend down and pick it up so he just left it there. 'Give us a packet of fags too, Davy,' he cried, patting his pockets.

I brought him the whisky and tried to make sure that he didn't drink it raw by picking up the water jug to top up his glass.

'Say when,' I said, sluicing.

'Whoo ...' he said and pulled his glass out of the way so that some water splashed onto the floor.

I helped myself to his money, picking some of it up off the ground. He didn't have enough, but I decided to let it be. He plonked himself down on the seat and sprawled his rubbery legs all over the place.

'No luck?' I said to him.

He shook his head despondently and swigged at his whisky. He buried his head into his hands and he said something I didn't catch.

'You should go home and get some sleep, Crunch,' I advised like an old fellow.

He looked up at me through two big bloodshot eyes. 'Sleep!' he said. 'Do you know... Give a guess where I spent the last two nights? The last two nights now, mind you!'

I shrugged.

'In a Salvation Army house where you sleep in your clothes, shoes and all, for fear they'll walk out the door on you .... Me! Captain Crunch! A place full of tramps and bums who'd cut your throat if they thought you had anything on you.'

'Shhh .. .' I said, warning him that we were not alone.

'Fuck them. I don't give a monkey's about them. Go and fuck the lot of them. I've nothin' to do with them. Listen Davy.'

'What?'

'Never mind lookin' out there ... fuck them ... listen to me for once in your life, listen to me.'

'I'm listenin'. What?'

'How long do you know me? A long time, right? And have I ever what-do-you-call-it ... have I ever… told you anything that wasn't…. Listen, Davy, you shouldn't be.... You put fellas like me up on some sort of pedestal. You do. I know you do. Don't latch on to fellas like me, Davy Wolfe. I'm no ... I'm no what-do-you-call-it ... I'm no… I can't make everything alright for you ... I can't make ....' Here he had a bad bilious attack and a bout of the hiccups on top of it.

'Are you alright?' I asked him, a hand on his shoulder.

'I'm alright, leave me be,' he griped, and a few tears fell out of his eyes and slipped down the side of his face.

'Crunch, go home and get some sleep for yourself,' I said. 'And something to eat!'

He waved me away brusquely, trying to hide his tears, drying them discreetly with the back of his hand. Someone called for a pint then and I had to leave him there.

Crunch stole away while I was pouring the drink and I saw Lar Lyons, out of the corner of my eye, taking off Crunch's drunken swagger for the unshaven character with the pencil behind his ear.

'You're fuckin' well bad enough,' I said to him angrily when I got a chance.

Crunch spent the next few hours in The Hole In The Wall. Then he drank his way back up to The Small Hotel again, where he fell in with a lonely commercial traveller. They stayed there, drinking into the early hours, until George got fed up of the pair of them and shut up shop.

Crunch, a free tin of assorted biscuits under his oxster, staggered out into the hushed street and headed for home, bumping off walls, crashing into dustbins and leaning helplessly against lampposts and railings. It was still dark but the first signs of light appeared in the sky and the initial, fresh chattering of birds could be heard.

Going up Keyser's Lane he slipped on something slippery that sent him crashing into a batch of bins and boxes, scattering their noisy belongings. He lay motionless there in the dark, dazed from the fright and the fall. Blood trickled down his face. He cursed loudly and the sound of his own voice bounced and echoed off the walls in the narrow, lonely old laneway. He tried to climb to his feet but couldn't seem to manage it. He slipped back down again, scraping his face off the rough edged wall, moss clinging to his outstretched fingertips; and suddenly he was gripped by a tremendous fear. He had heard the story about old Jem Dobson who had fallen right here in this very spot and when they found him in the morning he was dead. Dead, lying there with his eyes open and everything! Crunch became breathless just thinking about it, the walls closing in around him so that he felt like a man who was stranded on a terrific height and afraid of his life that he was about to fall into an abyss, that someone was about to slyly tip him over the edge or scoop the ground from in under him. He didn't dare to call out for help. No, if there was somebody out there, and he felt sure that there was, then that person or thing meant to harm him, take advantage of his helplessness. Yes, there was someone out there right enough, an eye in the darkness of that hallway, a mouth smirking and baring its teeth. He could hear a scratching sound somewhere and gravel crunching beneath somebody's feet and the menacing tinkle of broken glass. He could see his own distorted face in the end of the upturned biscuit tin and his heart pounded so hard that he honestly feared it was going to give his whereabouts away. He tried to rise again in vain, falling down and hitting the back of his head off the ground this time. Then there was a voice and someone helped him to his feet, a baker on his way to work more than likely, or a milkman maybe. Crunch shook himself free and, with the Samaritan duly rebuffed and banished, he staggered off up the winding laneway.

It was bright now and the glaring whiteness of the early morning nearly blinded him. He tried to convince himself that he was fine, that it was stupid to worry about something that wasn't there, but when he heard footsteps coming from a nearby street he stopped in his tracks and waited for them to recede and die away.

He finally made it to his own front door, a dingy second floor flat opposite Rowe Street chapel yard. He fumbled for his key and hurried inside, banging the door shut behind him with the hunted air of a frightened fugitive. He was sweating. And cold, freezing cold. He backed away from the hall door and stumbled backwards up the stairs, holding on for dear life to the shaky banisters. When the letterbox rattled he stood stock still on the landing and literally trembled. A faraway, mesmerising tune was beginning to take hold. Slowly, stealthily, he negotiated the landing, the floorboards making mocking music beneath him. He was outside his own room and half afraid to go in. Warily he pushed the door ajar and made a desperate lunge for the bed, it squeaked and protested beneath his dead weight. He knew that he should have closed over the door after him but he was unable- or unwilling- to rise up again to do it. The walls throbbed in and out like the sides of a melodeon. That crazy tune swirled round and round in his head, a wild fairground melody. What's it called? That tune? Tiny beads of sweat stood out on his forehead and cascaded down into his mad, misty eyes. He tried to cough. He began to shiver. Dun De Dun Dun Dun Dun Dee Dun Dee Dun Dun Dee Dun... He pulled his legs up around him and hugged his knees. Cold! That draught from the bottom of the what-do-you-call-it...window sill...Christ!...*Telestar*! That's it...*Telstar*...Dun Dun Dun Dun Dun Dun Dun Dun Dun Dun Dun Dun...He tried to cover himself up with a blanket, but couldn't quite make it all the way. Ffff, the cold!...Dun Dun Dun Dun Dun Dun Dun Dun Dun... No, not *Telestar*. What-do-you-call-it... *Wheels!* That's it, fucking *Wheels!*....Dun Dun Dun Dun Dun Dun Dun Dun Dun.

I stood outside the hospital gates, taking in the stark grey serious building and its manicured lawns. An ambulance was parked outside and I could make out a few white figures jostling to and fro. I turned up my collar to shelter me from the drizzle as I marched up the avenue past the proud sycamores and the sad rhododendrons, dreading the thoughts of going in there. I had heard that Crunch was in a bad state, that this time he had gone too far. What if he was a babbling imbecile? What if there were tubes and things sticking out of him and blood dripping from him? I have no stomach for that kind of thing. Even the smell of a hospital makes me squirm. This was the way I was thinking as I waited in the reception for someone to show me the way.

An elderly lady was on her knees, polishing and cleaning the floor. A fag dangled from her mouth as she coughed and wheezed and spat into her bucket.

Jesus, she'd put you off your grapes, I couldn't help thinking and I turned my attention to the attractive nurse who was manning the reception.

'Yes .... No, he's doing fine,' the nurse was saying into the telephone. 'Honestly, he is…Well, I mean the normal period is six or seven weeks, so there's nothing unusual about that. Yes, I know that. I know. Yes. Mmn.... He's in what? Oh yeah, right. I see what you mean. OK, Mrs Doyle, sure leave it at that and we'll see ....' She indicated to me that there was somebody behind to escort me to the ward.

I turned and followed the orderly down the gleaming, polished corridor, stealing a last glimpse at the attractive nurse and nearly treading on the poor old woman's worn out hands.

'I'd say there's some hard cases in here,' I said to the porter as he silently acknowledged a few patients who were roaming around in their dressing gowns and slippers.

'You don't know the half of it,' he said through a set of clenched teeth. He showed me to the ward and pointed me in the right direction. I thanked him and inched my way from bed to bed, gawking in at the snoozing inmates. I found him in the last bed, covered up and sleeping. He looked old and fragile all of a sudden. I sort of coughed for attention and slowly he opened his eyes.

'How are you feeling?' I said, moving closer to sit on the edge of his bed.

'What?... Davy .... I thought it was.... How did you get here?' He looked really groggy and, without his teeth, gaunt and pale.

'Are they treatin' you alright?

'What? Yeah...You'd better get a chair, Davy. She'll ate you if she catches you sittin' on the side of the bed like that,' he said, and there was pain in his voice.

I stood up and went across to get a chair. I turned to find him wincing in agony and licking his dry, parched lips.

'Davy, get us a glass of water there,' he keened, doing his best to sit up. 'I'm not supposed to yet, but...I'll have to take another one of them tablets.'

'Right,' I said and went to fetch a glass of water for him.

When I got back, to my horror, I found him slumped over in the bed. His head hung loosely and his eyes and mouth were wide open. One of his hands dangled down outside the covers, the other one was on his heart: Captain Crunch was dead.

I was surprised how calm I was under the circumstances. I went across and laid the glass of water down on the bedside locker and then I looked around for a bell, searching behind curtains and screens. Then in a flash Crunch was sitting up in bed and laughing hysterically and trying to tell me through his slobbering laughter how he had once played that same prank on his old landlady and she nearly split him open with a frying pan for frightening her like that.

'Oh, you bastard,' I said and sat, weak with the fright, on a nearby vacant bed.

Some of the other patients who were in on it were laughing at me, sitting up in their beds and quaking with joy.

'You should have seen yourself,' Crunch was saying as he wiped the mirthful tears away. 'Your little face when you thought old Crunch had snuffed it,' and he had another little titter. 'Hey, where's me grapes by the way?'

'Do you know what you are?' I said and I tossed the parcel across at him.

'Hey, go easy, I'm not well,' he said and he tore open the paper and began searching for the essentials. He found a packet of cigarettes and winked at me in appreciation. 'Did you bring me any... you-know-what?' he whispered and he looked around for spies.

'No, I didn't. You're bad enough,' I said.

'What do you mean? They're after drainin' every drop of drink out of me. I'm as dry as a bone, boy. A pioneer!'

'Yeah, and a virgin too I suppose,' I said, letting on to be cross with him.

He smirked, recalling with glee the look on my face when I thought he was dead. He blew a contented ring of smoke and said, 'I saw you comin' up the avenue and for a minute there I felt sure it was The Little Saint In The Friary comin' to visit me.'

I threw my eyes to heaven.

'No, straight up though,' he continued. 'I said it to the lads, didn't I, Freddie? I said "Well fuck me here comes The Little Saint In The Friary to see me,"' and he gave another phlegmy laugh. 'Fair play to you though, Davy. You didn't let me down all the same.'

'Yeah well, I thought you were dying from what I was told.'

'Is that what they were sayin'?' he said, charmed with the news.

'Yeah, and I was afraid you'd come back to haunt me if I didn't come up and see you.'

'Too right I would. What were they all sayin' about me though, Davy? Were they all feelin' sorry for me and all, yeah?'

'They said you were only an aul' bollix.'

He gave it some thought and then he laughed, shaking his head and sniggering, 'The Little Saint!'

'You're fine and snug here all the same,' I said, taking stock of the place.

'Yeah. Did you see that big one downstairs?'

'Who, the big one on reception?'

'Yeah. She fancies me.'

'I'd say that,' I said in a doubtful voice.

'No, straight up though. She's crazy about me, honest to God. The boys'll vouch for that there. "Have you got everything you need, Captain?" she says to me here the other day.' Crunch, taking her off, joined his hands daintily and flickered his eyelids and put on a great fancy twang. '"No," says I to her like that and she stops to ask what it is I'm wantin'. "A good woman," says I, "and a big bottle of Johnny Walker whisky and I'll never leave this place. I'll be as happy as Larry here." says I. "Oh," says she, "the whisky is out of the question, whatever about the other thing," and she swaggers out, looking over her shoulder at me that way.' (Here Crunch imitated how she looked over her shoulder at him, smiling her big brazen smile.) 'That's a fact, Davy,' he assured me. 'Ask the lads about that.'

'We'll never get you home out of here so,' I said, picking up one of his books. "*The One-Eyed Virgin Of Mozambique*,' I read aloud.

'I'll soften that one's cough for her,' Crunch promised, puckering up his bushy eyebrows.

'Is this any use, Crunch?'

'What? Which one? Oh, *The One-Eyed Virgin*. Yeah, that's a right book, boy,' he said, emphasising with his fist that it was a horny book.

A jittery man shuffled up the aisle, glanced out the window and nervously nodded to the two of us as he hobbled back down to the other end again.

'Look at that half-loon where he is,' Crunch cribbed. 'He'll have the floor wore out walkin' up and down.'

'Aw sure I suppose the poor devil is in a bad way,' I said.

'He's no worse off than any of the rest of us,' Crunch barked. 'You don't see me paradin' up and down the room like that - and mutterin'. He's a three-quarters of a loon so he is.'

I had to laugh, hearing him crib like that and watching him smoke and admire the fag that was tweaked between his brown stained fingers.

CHAPTER FIVE

I don't know if I was actually in love with Kathy or not. Maybe I only thought I was, maybe there's no real difference between the two conditions, maybe one automatically means the other, I don't know. All I know is that I wanted to be with her every chance I got and all my spare time (which wasn't much now because we were up to our ears in the bar) was spent either with her or thinking about her. I met her at lunch times and tea times and sometimes in the afternoons. We'd hold hands and kiss and touch each other tenderly. And like most young lovers we invented our own language with private in-jokes that nobody else would understand; and when we danced she'd snuggle in real close to me, putting her hands inside my jacket and sometimes inside my shirt, and she'd whisper that she never wanted to dance with anybody else. I wanted everybody to see her and I went out of my way to introduce her to all the regulars: Johnny said that she was a grand little girl; Crunch said that she was too skinny; Forty Winks said he knew her da well and Joe Crofton told me that my father said he'd love to see me in the saddle and I didn't know whether to believe him or not.

Kathy and I must have had thousands of conversations during the next few months, but to tell you the truth I can only recall one of them. Perhaps we just had the same conversation over and over again. I don't know. Words, it seemed, were not all that important to us back then. I know it was late at night. I had just finished work and had slipped out to meet Kathy, who was waiting for me under the canopy of The Small Hotel. I left my poor mother behind to finish up for me. Johnny was singing *Walking My Baby Back Home* and Kathy was laughing at the way they were able to glide so seamlessly from one song into another. We bought chips and walked along the Quay. Rocky was there too, running along ahead of us, sniffing and cocking his leg and jumping up into my arms like a circus dog. We sat on the old wooden seat in The Crescent and Kathy told me that if you listened real hard you could actually hear the stars. She said that they kind of purred and sometimes they sort of crackled. I listened real hard, but I couldn't hear a thing.

The dark outline of the concrete promenade ploughed through the sea and the Black Man pointed its ebony finger skywards. I told Kathy that there was a seal out there somewhere, probably out around Useless Island. Tomorrow I knew that a couple of fishermen from Rowdy Row were going after it. They would hunt it down and kill it.

'Run seal, run while you've the chance,' Kathy cried softly.

So I explained to her that they had to do it. In a matter of weeks a seal could clear out the entire harbour. It would also damage their nets and boats, and with a crinkled nose she implied that she understood. She smelled of shampoo and toothpaste and a hint of her big sister's perfume. She said that the laws of the sea were cruel and I agreed. Then she made me promise that I wouldn't destroy Useless Island when I was rich and famous. She said that everybody needed a Useless Island, something that wouldn't change or go away the minute you turned your back on it, and I gave her my word that when I was rich and famous I wouldn't change a thing. I would present it to her instead. We would rename it **Kathy's El Dorado** and she could go out there every night and talk to the stars.

'Hey Wolfe, I'll tell your da on you,' a voice called out from the other side of the street.

It was Hickey. He was with that woman from Rosslare Strand who had come into The Shamrock looking for him a few days back. I waved across at him, and when Kathy said that he was a very attractive man, you know, I think I was a little jealous.

&

Mister Martin could have had his wish, he could have died and gone to heaven before his money ran out, but he changed his mind at the last minute and clung on to the wreckage. It all started in the chapel. He felt strangely hot and clammy, a feeling that didn't leave him all through the mass. Somebody was coughing annoyingly over on the far side and a woman spread her massive bottom repulsively all over the seat in front of him. He sat up most of the time, fearing that he was going to faint, and during the communion he nipped out a side door, making a feeble attempt to genuflect before he left.

Outside he felt a taut pain attacking his chest and he had to hold on to a telegraph pole for support. Gently he slithered to the ground, the breath (like a genie in a bottle he'd later describe it) leaving his body like a slow puncture. When mass was over, to his horror, a crowd gathered around him. Somebody loosened his tie and top button while the lady with the big bottom crossed the street to the corner shop and called for an ambulance. The doctor said that he was a lucky man to be alive. He didn't know that Mr Martin wanted to die. Nobody knew that. Nobody would have ever suspected that was the case, seeing how the old man fought so hard to hang on to whatever was left of his life. And so Mr Martin didn't die spectacularly as planned but was carted off to a nursing home instead where he lingered for ages until eventually, I assume, he just wasted away.

George brought us the news. Should he have died there and then most of us would have felt remorse, regretted it, stopped to think about him or slowed down at least. But, as it was, we were all too busy to care. We would ask about his health every now and again certainly, but apart from that there wasn't much we could do about it. Besides, I had my own problems. I was working all the time now. It was our busiest summer so far and my father kept pointing out that it would be a long dreary winter. Danny was lost without me. He used to mope around waiting for me after work, but by then I was always too weary to be any fun. Most of my spare time I spent with Kathy now anyhow, much to Danny's chagrin. He would sulk and point out to me that there was more than one fish in the sea. He would tell me things that Skeleton Delaney did to certain girls who had expressed an interest in meeting the Mutt and Jeff of Wexford, namely Danny Newman and Davy Wolfe, but I was too far gone for that kind of thing.

It was Danny who first happened on Mr Martin's lighter in Ned Stand's window, stuffed between a snuff box and a heart-shaped cushion for medals. He pointed it out to me and I went down to The Small Hotel and told George about it.

'It must have fallen out of his pocket when he collapsed that time,' George surmised and pledged to bail it out the very next morning.

But when he came into The Shamrock the following afternoon he sighed and told me that it was gone.

'What do you mean?' I said to him, pouring his bottle of stout.

'Somebody else must have bought it, I suppose.'

'Already!'

'What's that?' my father wanted to know, glancing up from his spread-out local newspaper.

'The lighter,' George said.

'What lighter?'

'Ah, Mr Martin's fancy yoke, you know the one with the dancer inside it.'

'Why, where was it?'

'It must have dropped out of his pocket when he took the turn outside the chapel that time. Whoever picked it up pawned it. Davy saw it in Stand's window, but by the time I got there it was gone.'

'Any idea who bought it?'

'Ned said he wasn't there when it was sold. He was out at Mrs Kearney's funeral and the young lad was looking after the place. Ned called him out but the young fellow said he didn't know the man who bought it at all.'

'Oh well, you may say farewell to that now so,' my father stressed, switching newspapers.

'Yeah. It's a pity, 'cause it would have cheered the poor aul' divil up no end,' George said, rooting through his pockets. 'Give your da a drink there too, Davy.'

'No, I'm alright George. It's too early for me,' my father said.

'I wouldn't mind but I had every intention of being outside the front door this morning before they opened at all, but unfortunately I got a last-minute phone call to go up and collect the boss. And to make matters worse the friggin' car wouldn't start either. Here yare, Davy....What do you think, Paddy?' George said, reaching across for the local rag.

'Oh, Wooden Arse again. If he don't pull two or three there today I'll throw me hat at it altogether,' my father said, studying form.

'I fancy that *Hells Bells* myself,' George said, and stretched across to point him out to my father.

'Gordon Glynt?' my father warned him.

'Yeah, I know that, but... I have this sneaking feeling,' George said with a cute wink.

'Mmn ... maybe,' my father conceded, unconvinced.

'God, that was terrible about that Brennan chap, wasn't it?' George said, glancing at the front page.

'What? Yeah, I see that there,' my father said. 'He threw himself off the bridge according to that.'

'Yeah. A nice enough chap too.'

'I can't place him at all.'

'Yes, you do know him,' George insisted. 'He drove the bread van for Whelans. A tall man, terrible thin. He was often in here.'

My father was shaking his head.

'He always drank with that big red-headed fellow from Carne. What's this his name is now?'

'Oh yes. Yes, I have him now,' my father said. 'He always drank white rum. Glasses of it, neat.'

'That's him. Sure that was half his problem I think. They found the body anyway. Or what was left of it I should say.'

'Yeah. Paddy Burke found it I believe.'

'Not a pleasant thing to happen on then,' George said and turned the page. '"*One-way street for Wexford. Next month we will see a trial run of a one-way street system on Main Street in Wexford town. This motion was passed unanimously at last week's Corporation meeting on Monday night.*" Do you know what, boy, there'll be lads driving backwards and everything trying to avoid goin' out of their way ... "*due to the increase in traffic over the last few years and the constant dilemma that drivers have to face on the narrow, impassable Main Street."* Well, that's a fact alright. It's hectic sometimes.'

'It'll never work,' my father said emphatically.

'Of course it's only a trial run,' George pointed out.

'Oh that's all,' my father corroborated.

'The bold Hickey looks well,' George declared and he held up a photograph of Hickey and Mary in the newspaper, cuddling into one another at some reunion.

'That's a strong line,' George said.

'Looks like it,' my father agreed. 'Hickey is in his second childhood, sure,' and he sang a few bars of *Why Must I Be A Teenager In Love.*

He would often tease Hickey with this song when Hickey and Mary were sitting on the soft seat holding hands. Hickey would just glance over at him and smile and Mary would be wondering what all the grinning and smirking was about and she'd puck Hickey to cut it out, sensing that he was making fun of her.

George went through the entire paper that way, reading out various headlines and we'd discuss them and move on and Mr Martin's lighter was well and truly forgotten. And indeed so was Mr Martin.

I felt sort of sorry for him really, knowing how he treasured that thing. If he had shown it to me once he'd shown it to me a thousand times. He would carefully hand it to me and make me examine it thoroughly, holding it up to the light one minute to see the little dancer twirl and pirouette, then down flat in my palm the next minute to see how she curtsied. He would tell me how he came by it, describing the girl who gave it to him and everything. Then, out of the blue, he would snap at me to give it back to him before I damaged it on him. I'd hand it over and he would pop it into the dinky cloth bag and slip it into his waistcoat pocket. I never recall seeing him use it. He always bought a box of matches to light his pipe and if you went to work it he'd quickly bellow, 'Hey go easy there,' and snatch it from you disdainfully.

Well, it was gone now, and with it the life that Mister Martin had grown used to. Still, little did we know, eh?

CHAPTER SIX

Rainy Days, November nights, slippery streets, sad broken sailors, pointless conversations and long grey afternoons. Dark hopeless evenings too: the accordion abandoned on the soft seat, the snug empty and bare, the stairs creaking with the browned-off ghosts of the past. My father spent most of his time in the cellar these days or crouched in the back yard, sorting bottles and lobbing helpful hints to George on the far side of The Small Hotel wall.

Johnny was on the wagon again; Crunch was down in the dumps; and Wooden Arse Clampton was on a losing streak, which left Joe Crofton penniless and disgruntled. I spent most of my time hanging around Nolan's Cafe or down in the smoky Boker Poker Club, watching the privileged hoodlums huff and bluff behind the glass partition that was out of bounds for the likes of us.

Kathy had given me the heave. She turned up one night with a sad face on her and gave me the bad news. She said that she was dying alive about me, but ... I don't remember what came after the 'but'. I felt as lonely as the man in the moon without her. Danny would puck me chapishly and try to cheer me up by telling me about Skeleton Delaney and his sexual adventures. I told him that Skeleton Delaney was only a maw mouth and that Danny was worse for listening to him.

On top of all this Rocky disappeared on me and I couldn't find him anywhere. I searched high and low for him - across the bridge, up in the Hilly Holly, down Slaughter House Lane, and out by Rainwater Pond and all the other places we used to go and the shortcuts we used to take. Three weeks later he was fished out of the old scummy pond at the back of the fire-brigade station. My father said that he probably mistook the green scum for grass and jumped right in; or else a crowd of chaps, trick-acting, might have thrown him in for a lark. My mother worried and fretted about how long he'd been there, struggling to get out. Somebody told us that they could hear a dog yelping but couldn't make out where it was coming from.

And so Wexford was woebegone and feeling sorry for itself and Useless Island's sullen face was squashed into the square, curtained windowpane of The Shamrock, mourning for me and my lot. Holly's Toy Shop announced the countdown to Christmas - eight weeks, seven weeks, six weeks. But we didn't believe it would ever arrive. November: the month of hard-luck stories.

&

Mary woke to the sound of rain drumming on her galvanised kitchen roof: *he's gone, he's gone, he's gone* it seemed to say as she flopped over on her side to face the window. A never-ending supply of fat, juicy raindrops coursed down the glass to form all sorts of dainty designs and maps and intricate mosaics as they tumbled and fell. Sometimes they looked like a herd of strange, hunchbacked creatures, or tadpoles that merged with other tadpoles to become these larger greedy creatures that instantly consumed each other, speeding all the time to the end of their own parallel universe with a swift, darting, deadly urgency.

Outside winter raged in Rosslare Strand. The sea spewed and spat and plunged against the shore. Like an angry savage it ploughed up onto the beach, attacking the surf-breakers and the man-made walls, shattering them in places. It splashed and vomited ugly foamy waves that chewed the banks and devoured the land chunk after collapsing chunk. Worried men could often be seen frowning and scratching as they gazed down at this biting bitter bitch that was literally eating the ground right from in under them.

The village was like a cemetery this weather and there was a constant harsh wicked wind blowing in from the sea. The deserted corner shop refused to admit that anything had changed and outside on one of its makeshift stands some of the old stock was still on display: buckets and beach balls and carnival hats and what-not. At times the wind in the reeds almost piped a faintly familiar tune and there was a definite rhythm to the cloud of whipped-up grainy sand that pelted intermittently against Paddy Ryan's empty public house.

Mary put her hand behind her and felt the warm place where Hickey's body had carved out a deep empty ravine in the bed. She glanced across at her little boy who was playing away in his cot, contentedly gabbing and singing what could almost pass for a real song. She closed her eyes and her lips moved as if searching for some ancient, long-forgotten spell. She flapped onto her back to look up at the cobwebbed ceiling that bevelled down into her cosy living-room area. This was her pride and joy: a chintz sofa, a table with a bowl of artificial flowers standing on a round, white laced napkin; a portable black-and-white television set in the corner; and even her own kind of library, which was literally just a few Mills and Boon books on a Formica cabinet.

This might not seem much to most people, nothing to shout about or write home about or anything like that, but to her it was everything, a compilation of her life so far you might say - all the bumpy-ups and tumbling-downs, all the detours, all the heartache. She had found this place herself and done it up on her own, lugging and dragging and scraping and painting, and scouring the car boot sales and the second-hand shops for good-buys and bargains; and now as she looked out upon it all, the warm, satisfied glow that she'd usually felt was hindered or hampered, or whatever the word is, by the sound of the rain telling her, '*he's gone, he's gone,*' and the local church bell seemed to sound a far off farewell-thee-well to love.

She wished more people could see her place, she really did. She wished more people would drop in on her just to say hello and that kind of thing. But she knew that she was not the kind of person that you'd go out of your way to get to know, she was not interesting to talk to or anything like that. No, by nature she was a fairly withdrawn person, a trait that can be grossly misunderstood she often felt. Some people assumed that she was shy and just let her be. Others, however, she was sure, were convinced that she was an out and out dolt who was totally uninterested in anyone but herself. And she was often thought to be hard or cold or of no real significance at all. In any case her manner seemed to put people off and turn them away and all her life she had been punished for something that was as natural and irreparable as an impediment or a birth mark.

Mind you the photograph on the mantelpiece did nothing to dispel the myth - those two fiery eyes and that hard-headed look and that pouting, sullen mouth. A man would need to look long and hard to find the Goddess within she had to admit, he'd have to beat his way through the brambles and briars to get to the castle alright, no doubt about it. And even then she wouldn't give her heart too easily. No, she'd been short-changed and diddled out of her love too many times before for that. Her last man, she always maintained, was *'lost at sea'*, meaning that he got on board a big ship and never returned. And before that there was another joker who hitched a ride in a truck. She could still picture him climbing up into the lofty cabin, enthusiastically waving to her as he went freewheeling over the horizon, never to be seen again. And every time a man walked out on you like that he took with him a big bite out of your heart so that if you kept loving and losing that way very soon there would be none of you left.

Through the corner of her eye she discerned the spot where Hickey normally placed his black overnight bag, conveniently close to the door. The space was empty now. She turned her head away so that she would not see, but the germ of doubt had gained ground and taken root and the rain continued its sad refrain.

Last night he had cradled her in his arms in this very bed and they had laughed in the dark. Not that feeble thing that most people call laughter, real laughter that sprang from that other place. And then she had to go and tell him that she loved him. She shouldn't have done it. She should have known better than to spring something like that on a man like Hickey. She should have let it sink in gradually, let it dawn on him by degrees. The moment she said it she realised that she had committed the cardinal sin. Almost immediately there was a complete evacuation of warmth and tenderness from his body, from his face, from his fingertips and voice. There followed a short silent interval then so that their recent bout of laughter seemed to belong to some other realm. And then he told her that he didn't want to get in too deep, that maybe things had gone too far already, that she deserved a steadier fellow than him. Men always become rogues she noticed when they are trying to worm their way out of love.

Mary sat up in bed and confronted the empty space. The bag was definitely there last night, she was sure of that. Well, it wasn't there now. It was gone and with it another chunk of her heart. She closed her eyes, took a deep breath and listened. *He's gone ... he's gone ... he's gone*, the rain proclaimed. So much so that she let slip a few choked words. 'He's gone,' she said and her little boy, under the impression that she was talking to him, raised his arms to get out of the cot.

In the distance she heard the lonesome whistle of a locomotive, the train that would take Hickey back to town and his dreary room above Ned Stand's Pawnshop. She placed her hand inside the blankets and felt the outline of the Caesarean scar that knifed her body. It looked raw and ugly in the light of day and suddenly she began to take note of all the other things that were wrong in her life: this place was far too small for starters, and her stuff was either too dull or too gaudy or too cheap looking. Yes, her life was like some old sad Country and Western song: the kitchen roof leaked and the rent was already three or four days overdue.

و

It was in the Boker Poker Club that I saw it change hands. Danny was playing a game of snooker with an impish Cockney brat by the name of Quarry, and riding on the outcome was our last pound note, which we had pooled together in a shit-or-burst effort to get to the dance.

I watched the game eagerly, egging Danny on from shot to shot, saying, 'Nice shot,' and, 'Lovely Danny,' every now and again. Every so often my eyes would stray behind the tiny glass panel of the *'member's only'* back room where the shady elite of the town sat around a dimly-lit poker table. They all had their own special places to sit and their own style of smoking and spitting and their own peculiar habits when folding or dealing a deck of cards. The rusty old potbellied stove glowed like a furnace in the corner as the contrary, watery-eyed caretaker opened the lid to warm his hands - palms, fists and fingers. As he did so he worked his jaw like he wanted to say something that wouldn't be said or as if he was chewing something that refused to be swallowed. A bare bulb hung down over the card table while the rest of the room was mysteriously veiled and shadowed. I was intrigued as my very own gangster film reeled before me. What must I do to get inside that room? What daring deed must I accomplish before I am allowed to open the forbidden door? Skeleton Delaney was the only boy our age who ever went in there. He used to do messages for the men, and one night he said they let him sit in on a game.

And then I saw the lighter changing hands. Dancer picked it up and examined it, his strange eyes (one of his eyes was a different colour than the other) sneakily darting about: from the lighter to the man to the door. He mauled the little ballerina and fingered her between the legs. The bald man sitting opposite him - on a losing streak by the looks of things - flashed a seasick smile and half-heartedly laughed (overdoing it) at nearly everything the other men were saying. And with that Dancer gestured that he would accept the lighter in lieu of whatever money he was owed and he used it to light up the butt of a cigarette and then with a trickster's sleight-of-hand he slid the lighter out of sight. I couldn't take my eyes off him, and once, when he seemed to look directly at me, I dropped my head and turned aside just in case he remembered the fight in the bar that night. It turned out that he wasn't looking at me at all but at Skeleton Delaney who was signalling to him about something else entirely.

Then Danny tossed his cue across the table indignantly and snatched his jacket off the coat rack. He had lost the game and was angry at himself for letting us down. He headed straight for the door, beckoning with his head for me to follow. I dawdled there awhile, wondering what to do about the lighter, and then I reluctantly followed Danny outside.

'Well, that's that,' he said when I arrived on the scene. 'A waster! I mean I should have whitewashed him. I wouldn't mind but I had every chance too.'

'Never mind,' I said, trying to console him.

'There goes the dance,' he lamented.

'Listen, do you know what I just saw in there?'

'What?'

'Mr Martin's fancy lighter.'

'Where?'

'Dancer has it. He won it off your man with the bald head.'

'Who? Oh, Yul Byrne.... Well, you may say goodbye to that now so.'

'Maybe he'd sell it back to us,' I suggested.

Danny eyed me sideways. 'With what?' he said. 'We haven't a button between us and you want to try and do a deal with the biggest chancer in town. Forget it!'

'I could get the money off George.'

'Yes you could, yeah!... Look the only one worrying about that yoke now is you. I'd say even Mr Martin is after forgettin' all about it at this stage. Leave it be, Davy. It's well and truly out of reach now anyway.'

'No, I'd say George would come up with the money alright,' I reasoned.

'Yeah well, you tell George to go and get it back then. That Dancer is a madman and I don't want to have anything to do with him,' Danny said and walked away, shaking his head in bewilderment at the very idea of me worrying about an old lighter when our last pound note had just gone by the board.

🪝

The next few weeks, although quiet, were not without their share of happenings. Joe Crofton grew a beard and won himself a nice crisp fiver when a plumber down from Dublin bet him that it wouldn't grow in a month. Joe Crofton grew a beard every winter and knew exactly to the last hair how long it would take.

My father spent most of his time worrying and figuring. He was fairly narky and quick to snap at me if I put a foot astray. I cursed him into a knot behind his back saying, 'It's not my fault that business is slack.' My mother told me that he was just worried, that he was afraid he would end up losing the pub and have to go back to England again. I warned her that if he didn't lay off me that I would be the one to go away to England.

One day I watched him fidget and fumble in his office (the snug). I heard his calculating cough and I knew that something was afoot. Soon I was summoned to find him licking three large brown envelopes. With these I was dispatched and given the strict instruction that I was to wait for a reply. When I asked the simple question: 'What's in them?' I was nearly devoured.

Of course I knew exactly what was in them: bills; money owed by lousers who now avoided The Shamrock at all costs. My father was forever giving out and complaining about this sort of fellow. 'You not only lose the money you loaned them but you also lose their custom,' he'd say to George late at night and George would silently agree and mumble, 'That's a fact alright.'

However, I tried not to show in my face or my reaction the least inkling of hesitation or alarm and so I just took the letters from him, stuffed them into my coat pocket and nonchalantly rambled out onto the street. The plan was the same as always: stuff them under the door and beat it.

Outside, I took a peek at the addresses - one was in John Street, one was in Hill Street and the third one was up in Rowdy Row. I'd leave that until last (life is precious). I met Crunch on my travels. He was standing on the corner and gazing moodily out to sea. First off he wondered with two pleading eyes if I had any money to spare. I shook my head, stretching out my hands haplessly. Then he eyed the envelopes, which were jutting out of my pocket.

'Pony Express,' I told him. 'Bills. Anyone and everyone who owes us money will be brought to court and tried by a jury of his own peers.'

'Tell him I'll fix him up Tuesday,' he said. 'Or Wednesday, rather. I'm expectin' a cheque,' Crunch asserted and added gruffly, 'I don't want no bills, I'm tellin' you that now for nothin'.'

'What? Yeah,' I said, hiding the addresses from him, 'I have one for you alright,' I lied just to annoy him.

'Look, I don't want no bills,' he griped, letting on to be exceptionally harangued by the whole affair.

He tagged along with me, for want of anything better to do. We took care of John Street and then Hill Street before setting out for the long trek up to Rowdy Row. Crunch lagged behind me most of the time, gasping and begging me to slow down a bit. I couldn't help thinking about all the times me and Mickey Fury would wind up here when we were boys. I had an uncle who lived in Rowdy Row and I was, from time to time, sent up to deliver some message or other. It used to take us hours on end to get there. We would dally through the Saturday streets of Wexford, taking the longest shortcuts we could find. Up halcyon cul-de-sacs where the well-off elite lived and we'd laugh at the sight of a bubble car or steal a squint in at some rare sight such as a television in the parlour or a phone in the hall. Then we'd climb over somebody's wall and stroll lackadaisically across a bumpy field, stopping to gaze down at the lonely convent below. And Mickey would never fail to say something about the nuns who shut themselves up and prayed their lives away. We'd pass the presbytery and the two of us would salute like soldiers at the sight of a priest standing in the manse doorway. Up sleepy avenues and side streets, a quick glimpse in at the handball alley, and then maybe we'd dodge down some smelly lane after calling out and making fun of poor harmless Victor.

When we finally reached Rowdy Row, Mickey Fury and me that is, our jaunty stride would falter and our gaiety would quickly subside. We'd tiptoe across that angry playground like two cowboys inching across a sacred Indian burial ground. Invariably the gap at the other end would be blocked by a gang of freckle-faced boys who normally frowned on strangers. We'd trade glances, tough defensive glances, and sometimes we'd swap wisecracks and insults. Ingenious things like, 'Who knitted your face and dropped a stitch?' We had learned over the years not to humour them or to try and get in with them by acting all innocent or asking real down-to-earth questions because no matter what you said it would be misconstrued or deliberately misunderstood anyway and you'd end up in worse trouble than you were in at the start. So we learned to give as good as we got. Sometimes we would just go on by and other times we'd have no other option but to stand our ground and one of us - usually me for some reason- would be called upon to fight. Once I recall getting the tar beaten out of me by a little furious fellow and a passing man had to pull us apart. Another time, to my surprise (for after all this was the other side of town), I ended up knocking the stuffing out of my opponent, I think I may even have reduced him to tears.

In any case win, lose or draw we always came home a different route. We would climb down the grassy bank that led to The Shelter where the fishermen worked, our bellies stuffed with fancy cake and biscuits that my Aunt Alice would dish up for us. We'd stand and watch the men dragging their barnacled boats in close to the shore and we'd marvel at the world that they took for granted: the crabs that crawled out of the rutted tracks the dragged-in boats had left behind, the wheeling seagulls that scooped down like big vultures to devour the fish that were not needed, the sloshing of the sandy-heeled boots clouding the lonely orphan pools the out-going tide had forgotten. The fishermen were alien to us too, their sturdy bodies bloated up with the layers of jumpers they wore and their faces devoid of any humour, as if it was a sign of weakness or something: big bulky men with strong arms, stumpy tattooed manikin men with serious frowns, old mariners with wind-scarred faces. Once in a while one of them would recognise one of us and heartily cry, 'Well young Fury, how's your da?' or 'Young Wolfe me old son,' which of course would make our day. But most times they'd ignore us and go about their work, bickering and complaining.

I'll never forget the day we tumbled head-over-heels down the slippy cliff and into a cluster of sting nettles at the bottom. (What age were we then? Ten or eleven maybe.) A hefty boy, who was supposed to be helping his father paint a boat or some such thing, found this hilarious and laughed at us and called us a right pair of ejits. We ignored him as best we could, doctoring the blisters with dock leaves and spit.

'Go away ye pair of gobshites,' he shouted across at us.

'Come over here and say that,' I said over my shoulder, much to Mickey's consternation.

'What did you say?' the big boy said, dropping the paint brush and heading towards us, obviously surprised that a little runt like me would have the neck to give him impudence. 'What did you say to me?' he said again, coming closer.

'I said come over here and say that,' I repeated, and the two of us laughed and smirked nervously.

'I said you're a **right... pair... of... gobshites**,' he said, jabbing me with his finger, enunciating every insulting word like a bully in a cartoon.

I looked askance at Mickey, who was wondering what my next move would be and getting ready to make a run for it. Until I piped up with burlesque amusement, 'Fair enough. I couldn't really hear what you were saying from over there, like you know.' I said, and we strolled away tittering, leaving him, I'm relieved to say, baffled and bewildered.

But on this day with Crunch it was not like that at all. He and I swaggered across the unkempt playground undaunted. Crunch was unimpressed with Rowdy Row and its reputation. He told me that he had seen places so rough they would make Rowdy Row look like a kindergarten. And I showed him a spot where I once held a girl, telling Crunch about it, exaggerating the incident.

'Who? You did?' Crunch said, smiling. 'Where? Over there?' and he began to laugh, analysing my story, sifting out the lies, paring it back to the truth, liking the sound of it. 'Ha ... ha ... Aw Davy, you know what, you're the only one that can make me laugh sometimes, you know that, don't you? But you be careful, boy. I'd hate to see you get yourself in any kind of trouble. I'll kick the arse off you if you do, I'm tellin' you that here and now for nothin'.'

Now it was my turn to laugh.

He halted in his tracks then and took a long serious look at me. 'I'm terrible fond of you, boy,' he said softly. 'I know I'm a queer hawk and all the rest of, but ....There's people I like and there's people I don't like and the people I like I like and the ones I don't like...well...fuck 'em...' and here he sort of shrugged and indicated that he had run out of words of wisdom and with that we carried on into the heart of Rowdy Row.

Crunch stopped to talk to Easy Going Larry, telling me to go on about my business, that he was wore out and too weary to go any further.

'Give us a fag, Crunch,' were the first words that escaped from Easy Going Larry's lips.

'I'll give you a box in the friggin' forehead!' I heard Crunch exclaim as I walked away from the pair of them.

When I returned, after furtively slipping the envelope under the door, I found Crunch and Easy Going Larry in conversation about Dancer. Easy Going Larry was saying that Dancer had threatened to put a brick through The Shamrock window (Crunch told me this afterwards because as soon as I showed up Larry shut up like a clam) and Crunch said that he told him that if he did he'd be one sore boyo because Paddy Wolfe was one hardy bit of stuff.

What happened after that was like something from a Laurel and Hardy picture. A crowd of lads who were playing football close by called for me to kick the ball back to them. I did and it was only over there when they were calling again, 'Hey Mister, give us the ball back,' and Crunch, full of vim and vigour, burst through, pretending to be in Croke Park or somewhere, hunching me aside with his shoulder and holding the ghost of other players at bay as he picked up the football. Then with a wild cry he let it rip, the ball Garryowening up over our heads. It landed with a crash, smashing through a plate glass window.

'That's it, I'm off,' Easy Going Larry said and bailed out, calling over his shoulder as he vanished, 'That's Maureen 'Custard' Murphy's house.'

All the little boys had already run for cover. They jumped over hedges and cleared walls with a single leap. They hid behind cars and down behind dustbins. From this I gathered that Maureen 'Custard' Murphy took no prisoners and I decided we should make a hasty retreat. I led the way, heading for our old escape route. As we climbed down the grassy bank Crunch took an awful tumble. Behind us we could hear some commotion and we both knew that it wouldn't be long before she was on our trail.

'Look at the state of me,' Crunch moaned, standing up and wiping his clothes, which were destroyed. 'Will you hurry up before we're lynched,' he bawled as I picked my way carefully down the mucky slope.

Then there was a ferocious shriek from above and I looked around to see a banshee glaring down at me.

'Here youse, that's a brand-new window and if youse tink now for one minute now that a pair of tinkers like youse are goin' to... .'

I made a jump for it when I saw Crunch darting away. I passed him out and left him for dead as he stumbled awkwardly - long loping strides and hysterically laughing - along the railway tracks. When I reached the deserted station I stopped to let him catch up on me again.

'I think we've lost her,' I said, scanning the horizon.

'What's that?' Crunch panted, sitting down on the platform for a rest.

'It's alright,' I said. 'We've lost her.'

'I wouldn't bank on that,' Crunch said. 'She won't give up that easy or anything. Here take a peek over that wall there and see if there's any sign of her.'

We went across to the wall, where Crunch cupped his hands together and gave me a hooch up. From my human crow's nest I had a clear vista of Trinity Street and most of William Street too. The tiny squat houses opposite looked contented, smoke billowing out of their fat chimneys. A woman in an apron was at her door chatting to an insurance man, who then rubbed his hands together and moved along to the house two doors up. Some men who were working on the road were having a cup of tea in their caboose and calling out to the postman who happened to be passing. And then I saw her, pedalling hell-for-leather down the hill and looking like Old Mother Reilly on a high Nellie bike.

'I knew that,' Crunch cried half to himself when I put him in the picture. 'Lord God almighty, the trouble you get me into.'

'You kicked the ball,' I reminded him.

'Look, never mind that,' he said, and pondered.

'We could say that we weren't next or near the ball,' I proposed.

Crunch shook his head.

'We could offer to pay for the broken window,' I went on.

This was even less acceptable.

'We'll have to do something. She's goin' to cut us off at the other end,' I harped.

'I know what we'll do,' Crunch said, tapping his wily temple.

He led me into the gasworks yard where all the workmen and even the manager eyed us suspiciously. Crunch was grinning and waving like a politician and urging me to keep going. We eventually came out of there and he led me into The Talbot Hotel. Here he suggested we have a quick slash, which we did. Then out through a different door and soon we were on Main Street and mingling with the parading shoppers and Crunch, feeling secure now, slapped my back and laughed again. He jumped up in the air, grabbed an imaginary ball and kicked it away from him, screeching, 'Over the bar says Lowry Mar.'

Meanwhile, I, for my part, let on not to be with him.

We went striding up Main Street and Crunch stopped to talk to a few men who were loitering on a street corner. A few minutes later he caught up with me again, a cigarette in his mouth, and the finicky man inside the jeweller's shop turned away insolently from Crunch's hoodwinking wave. When I smiled at a girl that I sometimes danced with I noticed that she went red, a sign that maybe she secretly fancied me. A lanky cop stood in the mouth of Keyser's Lane chatting up this grand attractive woman. Crunch said hello to her and I was surprised when she knew his name and everything.

We were soon in the rumbling bowels of Wexford, the smells and sounds of the street vying and blending and fighting for domination: the overwhelming smell of the laundry, the awesome sound of chopping as we passed a butcher's shop, the lilting music of a girl's voice calling up to her flatmate to throw down the key; the delicious aroma of fresh bread wafting from Kelly's bakery, the street sweeper's swept-up pile, a glimpse of the sea every now and again, hardware shops and grocery shops and steaming cafes, and the quaint grey Protestant chapel bell clanging in the middle of the afternoon.

We wandered into The Bull Ring, both of us hailing some old timer who greeted us with, 'Nippy enough,' and for peace sake we both agreed with him even though we were sweating. There was Johnny's Shoebox and Ned Stand's Pawnshop and the market gates thrown open and Maureen 'Custard' Murphy laying down her bicycle against the Pike Man monument.

I pointed her out to Crunch and he hushed up my noisy nodding and suggested that we tiptoe across and take refuge in Johnny's place. Meanwhile she was manoeuvring around the square, sniffing and spying. We hid behind the monument and when Crunch gauged that the time was right we made a desperate dart for it. We didn't make it all the way, however. She turned around and we were forced into Ned Stand's doorway. Crunch tried the door furiously. It was locked. There was a sign on the door, which read: **GONE TO LAR DOYLE'S FUNERAL.**

'The curse of the seven snotty orphans on Lar Doyle and all belonging to him,' Crunch said, peeping out and seeing her gawking into Johnny's window.

'Quick, next door,' I suggested and we nearly knocked one another down as we made a bee-line for the barber's shop.

Joe Shiggins, a sour-faced merchant at the best of times, didn't take too kindly to us barging into his place like that. He stopped what he was doing and scowled across at us.

'Hello Joe,' Crunch said, matter-of-factly.

Joe turned away, saying curtly, 'I'll be with you in a minute,' and he went back to work.

'No hurry, Joe,' Crunch said sitting down, beckoning for me to do the same.

I was reluctant to sit down in this shop for fear that Shiggins would get any notions about scalping me. When I was a boy my father would always send me down here to have my hair cut. I used to have to take the back streets home after Shiggins got through with me. I would see my reflection in shiny windows, or watch my shadow with jagged spikes of hair sticking up, and pointed ears, which I'd never realised belonged to me. I'd curse Joe Shiggins for making a holy show of me and vow to hibernate for a month or two. Later on, when I got a bit older, I used to try and tell Joe exactly how I wanted it cut. 'Leave it over the ears,' I'd say, 'and give me a neck shave too.' Then I'd watch his old shrivelled-up face in the mirror, smiling a sort of leering smirk as if he was happy enough to be told what to do. But you could tell by his narrowed eyes that he was raging. The cheek of me to tell him how to cut my hair, an impudent pup who would be taught a lesson, and I would be duly crucified with reams of hair and curls shuttle-cocking all over the shop.

And there he was now, the last of the Mohicans, snipping away at this old man's hair and gazing out over his DeValera glasses at the jittery boy who was pacing up and down his shop and anxiously looking out the window. I decided to sit down when I realised that my standing and pacing annoyed him. In the wink of an eye he'd put you out.

'How's that, Bob?' he asked, taking a good look at the man in the chair through the mirror.

'That's grand, Joe,' your man said, too shy to take a really good look at himself.

'Brylcreem, Bob?'

'Please, Joe. Just a… little,' Bob said, but it was a trifle too late, Joe had already smothered him.

Then with skilled virtuosity Joe found the parting and slicked back Bob's head of hair so that he looked like an Italian gigolo. And then Joe patted and touched and moulded Bob's hair into its natural position, whipping out combs and brushes, which, along with the other tools of his trade, filled up the pockets of his long white coat. And when his eye caught mine in the mirror I looked away and let my gaze take in the rest of his pomaded shop with its ointments and creams and concoctions: the crude sharpening belt that dangled down and looked like a Christian Brother's strap, the dry shampoos and lotions and the shelves full of crispy towels and flannels and cards of combs for sale. On the wall there was a poster of a friendly barber slicking back some handsome man's hair. Underneath the poster there was an open fire that crackled and smoked every time the door was opened or closed. There was a Sacred Heart lamp glowing in the corner and the bare floorboards that would creak out the next customer and there was the smell of soap and the air was spiked with the musty scent of all the mouldy magazines that had built up over the years.

'OK, Bob?' Joe said, taking off the sheet and shaking it clean.

'Lovely job, Joe,' Bob said and fished into his pocket for his money.

'All the girls will be after you now, Bob,' Joe joked. 'Ain't that right, Denny?'

'What's that, Joe?' old deaf Denny said.

'I say all the girls will be after him now.'

'Yeah, that's right,' Denny agreed, struggling to his feet and breathlessly toddling over to take his turn in the barber's chair.

'Aw, the aul' bone is broke, lads,' Bob said, waiting for his change.

'The same as meself, Bob. And six pence for yourself. Thanks very much, Bob,' Joe said. Then a look of perplexity shadowed his face and he muttered under his breath, 'Who the hell is that foggin' up my window?'

It was Maureen 'Custard' Murphy and she had her nose pressed up against the window, trying to see inside. Crunch and I hid behind two upside-down magazines. Joe went right up to her and pulled the blind down in her face.

'That one should be certified,' he said, and switched on the light.

'Who's that, Joe?' Bob said as Joe helped him into his top-coat.

'Oh, that Healy one. You know the one from Rowdy Row. Maureen Healy. Murphy is her married name.'

'God, I can't place her at all,' Bob said, pulling back the blind and peeping out.

'Yes, you do know her, Bob,' Joe said. 'They call her Custard Murphy. I don't know why. She looks more like a crab apple to me.'

'Is it safe for me to go out there yet?' Bob wondered.

'What? Oh, work away, Bob. And listen don't forget you can only go the one way from now on up that Main Street now.'

'What, even on me bike?'

'Even on your hoop, Bob.'

'That's scandalous,' Bob said from the doorway.

'It's madness so it is, Bob. Madness,' Joe concurred.

'Aw sure what harm, lads. I was only goin' to go the one way anyway,' Bob laughed and disappeared out the door.

'Good man, Bob,' Joe called after him, the rusty bell sounding.

In the split second that the door was ajar I spied the queer one still hunting the Bull Ring for us. I looked at Crunch and he motioned that he had seen her too and we settled back for a long wait.

'Well, Denny, the usual is it?' Joe was saying, wrapping him up in the sheet.

'Yeah. A bit off all round,' Denny said, which was amusing since old Denny only had a handful of hair left.

But Joe didn't even flinch. He carried on as if Denny was a young fresh-faced youth with a powerful head of hair. He combed it, studied it, wetted it, stood back and surveyed it and eventually set to work on it.

Just then the door opened and my heart leaped with the fright. Crunch grabbed hold of my elbow and was sitting on the edge of the seat and getting ready to make a break for it. It turned out to be a red-faced farmer who put his head around the door and inquired, 'Where's your back, boss?'

Joe looked across at him as if he was hearing things. 'The what?'

'The back? The lav?' the farmer pleaded.

Joe didn't give things away like that and he was in no hurry to loan out his toilet to every Tom, Dick and Harry who happened in off the street and so he told the farmer - who was not even a regular customer of his - in no uncertain terms where to go and what to do.

'Huh, the cheek of him,' Joe said when the door was closed and old Denny made a face in the mirror. 'Tell us, Denny, did you ever get to Rome after all? The last time you were in you were sayin' something about ...'

'I did, yeah. God, I did, Joe. And we had a right time out there,' Denny said, keeping a close eye on Joe's activities in the looking glass.

'And how is the daughter?'

'She's in right form, thanks be to God,' Denny assured him. 'And the husband is a grand chap too. Their home is only out of this world, that's all's about it. Out of this world so it is.'

'Go away out of that. And, ah... tell me this and tell me no more... Is that alright for you, Denny?'

'Oh, that's grand, Joe. Sure you're the boss.'

'Ah, what was I goin' to say?,...Oh yeah, what does your man work at, Denny?'

'Who's that? Oh, Franco. Franco has a right job, Joe, so he has. What they call continental hours where you work only when it suits you sort of thing and as long as you get your work done it doesn't matter what time you come and go at, you know.'

'Yes, begor. That would never work here, Denny.'

'No. I wouldn't think so, Joe.'

'But what does he do exactly?'

'Who?'

'This Franco character?'

'Who?'

'Franco. Your daughter's husband,' Joe snapped testily.

'Oh .... he works in the Vatican,' Denny crowed and there was a reverent pause with the barber practically on the verge of genuflection.

'The Vatican?' Joe repeated, looked our way and gave a soft, impressed whistle. 'And I don't suppose you got inside it at all, no?'

'What? God, I did, Joe. Sure I was in and out of it by the new time, man. Nearly every day; every second day anyway!' Denny said.

'I'd say that's a fairly expensive place then, Denny, is it?' Joe said, angling for more information.

'Stop the noise. Fifty pounds it cost me for a meal one night. I took the lads out to dinner one night, you know to kind of make up to them for being so generous all through the holiday. 'Cause Franco wouldn't let me put my hand in my pocket, Joe.'

'A decent lad, was he?'

'Oh, the best,' Denny said and gave a little affected cough.

'It's not like them foreigners to be so givish with their money then.'

'No. But this lad was different, Joe. He was like an Irishman.'

'Yeah, I know what you mean, Denny,' Joe said, going around the other side of the chair. 'But fifty pounds was a bit steep, Denny.'

'Fifty pounds it cost me. And for nothin' special either, Joe. I mean there was nothin'… elaborate about it or anything.'

'Do you hear that lads,' Joe said, involving us. 'Fifty pounds he spent on a dinner. And he's a mean man. Just imagine what it would cost a decent bloke. Oh, I think I'd go hungry before I'd spend fifty pounds on me dinner, lads, would you? Fifty feckin' smackers. I would in me granny! I would not. No way.' And then Joe winked at us and said, ' Tell us, Denny, did you happen to catch a glimpse of the Pope at all and you over there?'

'Catch a glimpse of him? I met the man,' Denny said, and nearly got his throat cut for saying it.

'Aw now, Denny, you're not serious?'

'God, I am serious then,' Denny said, and when he saw the disbelief in Joe's eyes he perked up and swore blind that he had met the man in person. 'As true as I'm sitting in this chair tonight ... or this afternoon I should say,' and slowly Joe came around. 'I met the man face-to-face so I did. Franco arranged it, you know. It seems that once or twice a year anyone that works there can be granted an audience if they put in for it and wait their turn.'

'And you saw him up close?'

'As close as I am to you right now. Sure I shook his hand and everything. A lovely man, Joe. A gentleman.'

'Well, did he say anything to you, Denny?'

'What's that? Oh yeah, he did. We had a conversation alright,' he said, in no hurry to divulge the rest of his story.

'What did he say?'

'He said ah - just a small bit off the back, Joe. Give me one of those new what-do-you-call-its - 'em neck shaves,' Denny said, digressing.

'What? Oh yeah, right, Denny.'

'Where was I?'

'You were sayin' the Pope spoke to you. You were about to tell us what he ah ....'

'Oh yeah...'

Just then the farmer came in again and he was purple in the face. 'Is there no chance of using your back, boss?' he begged. 'I'm after being all over the place and I can't get in anywhere.'

'What? Yeah, go ahead,' Joe conceded and irritably waved him through. 'Sorry Denny, go ahead,' Joe apologised.

'What's that?'

'What did he say, Denny?'

'What did who say?'

'The feckin' Pope, God forgive me for cursing,' Joe said, his patience waning.

'Not much, Joe,' Denny said and gave his little affected cough again.

I felt like grabbing the old fucker by the lapels myself at this stage. He hemmed and hawed and was just about to start into it again when the farmer entered once more, fastening his fly and saying, 'Thanks very much. You're a gentleman so you are. I was dying to ...'

Joe turned on him savagely. 'Look, will you just get out of my shop,' he said, pointing towards the door and we all watched him depart, all three of us turning back to Denny when he was gone.

'Go ahead, Denny,' Joe sighed.

'I'll tell ye, lads, I never met a more ordinary down-to-earth man in all my life and I'm nearly eighty years of age. The first thing he said to me was, and I thought it was terrible nice of him, "Céad míle fáilte," he said. It warmed the cockles of my heart to hear it too, I don't mind admitting.'

'Yes, of course it did, Denny. The man was welcoming you in your own native tongue, your own language, céad míle fáilte, a hundred thousand welcomes,' Joe said as if he knew the Pope's form.

'I was brought then into a big room with a high ceiling and the Pope sat up on a kind of a throne,' Denny continued. 'I knelt down to kiss his ring ... and ... I'll never forget the look on his face, a sort of strange look, you know like there was something worrying him or something....'

'Yes, I know, Denny,' Joe consoled him, trying to keep the thing going now.

'And then he said to me ... eventually now ... not straight away or anything, you know. He said to me, "Dennis." I had been introduced to him as Dennis, you see.'

'What? Oh, yeah. Dennis. Yeah, Dennis Quigley. Of course. Your full name. Your proper name,' Joe said, well up on protocol.

'"Dennis,"' says he, "don't mind me asking you, but who in the name of God cut your hair? It's a holy show so it is,"' and Denny nearly fell out of the chair laughing.

Joe pretended to be amused at the prank, glancing and winking at us, his old dried-up mouth twitching in disgust.

'Oh, good man, Denny. That's one up for you alright,' he said as poor old Denny lost the last few remaining hairs he had left.

I turned to say to Crunch wasn't it a good one. He just shrugged it off and went over to the window and peeked out.

'Jaysus, there's Durango Clark, the very man I want to see,' he said and he rushed out the door and left me to my fate.

CHAPTER SEVEN

There was a gigantic Christmas tree erected in The Bull Ring with glitter and tinsel and all the usual paraphernalia adorning it. Christmas lights and decorations were festooned across the square and in Johnny's Shoebox window there was a big boot with make-believe frost all around it. The sign in Holly's Toy Shop said *JUST SEVEN DAYS TO XMAS* and the rosy woman inside smirked as if to say: *we told you so.* Victor stood beneath the tree, frozen to the bones and eyeing suspiciously anyone who came too near. He blended in well with the ginger headed travellers who were flogging mistletoe, sprigs of holly and knocked off Christmas trees. Cheap Charlie's voice called out and amused the cavalcade of people who filed past, and there was a pony and trap trotting up Main Street with Santa Claus on board, ringing a bell and enticing everyone towards Maxwell's Store. The Santa was about three sizes too small for his suit, which was clearly made for a roly-poly man. People were making guesses about who was inside the get-up.

I was sitting on the Pike Man monument, waiting for Danny. It was four o'clock in the afternoon and as was our tradition we were going on our annual ran-tan. Well, it wasn't exactly a tradition yet, but it would be in a few years time. Last year was our first outing. We went on a pub crawl and we had so much fun that I can recall little or nothing about it. I know we got drunk and I think we got into a sort of a fight which we must have either won or ran away from because neither of us had any black eyes or bruises or anything like that. This year I suspected would be no different.

The streets were crowded with people coming out of the shops, bearing bags and laden down with stuff, stopping to natter and disappearing, flushed and flustered, up various side streets. The railwayman led his big dray horse up the busy thoroughfare, holding on to the halter, hailing across to Victor who was saluting him like a soldier. Kathy was there too. She had her arm around this other boy, smiling up at him just like she used to smile at me. My heart sank to see her with somebody else. I was dying for her to come over and say something to me, but she didn't, she went on up the town and I knew I'd have to learn to live without her, that I was not going to win her back.

When Danny finally showed up he found me in a pensive mood. I think he thought that I was mad at him for being late. He told me that he had just come from the Boker Poker Club where he had won thirty bob from Quarry playing snooker. We tramped down to The Hole In The Wall, stopping to listen to a group of carol singers on the way, smiling in at a few girls we recognised. The plan was to drink our way up to The Shamrock without missing a single pub. We got off to a great start too. I called the old fellow Mister James when I was ordering two pints, and he turned turk on me and put us out. The next place refused to serve us as well, with the barman saying that we both looked under age.

'We're some hard cases, ain't we,' I joked. 'That's two already.'

'Yeah, *Mrs Brown you've got a lovely...*,' Danny sang, adopting a drunken stagger.

Eventually we did get served in a couple of places and by the time we reached The Shamrock things were more than a little hazy, from where I stood anyway. Danny was trying to break in a new pair of Beatle boots and they were cutting the ankles off him. In the end he removed one of them and I had a vague recollection of him see-sawing along behind me, calling for me to wait for him and me telling him over my shoulder to get a move on.

The Shamrock was thronged by the time I got there. Somebody bought me a drink, but I couldn't place who it was. Somebody else was laughing like a hyena somewhere, a wild infectious laugh that had everyone tittering and grinning and smirking all around him. I went searching for the maestro so I could offer to buy him a drink.

'Any man that can laugh like that deserves a free drink,' I kept saying to anyone who'd listen to me.

I couldn't find him anywhere. I was going right up to people, gazing into their faces, trying to get them to laugh, digging my finger into their ribs and that. I'm sure if I had been anyone else I'd 've been put out. At one stage somebody handed me a stick of chalk and told me to mark the board. I immediately obeyed even though I could hardly see the board. It was a fairly serious game of darts too, for turkeys, and there was I in the middle of it, making a hames of the job.

'What's that supposed to be? A hundred and what?' someone asked.

My writing was illegible. Nobody could make head nor tail of it, including me, so I was sacked on the spot. They had to scrap the game and start again. Everyone was black out with me. 'Go and sit down somewhere, Davy, out of that,' Durango Clark said, disgusted.

The next thing I knew I was standing alongside Lar Lyons and suspecting him of being the hyena. I watched his mouth, getting down in under him because he was three-sheets-to-the-wind himself and all bent over. My mother, who was up to her ears, considered asking me to give her a hand, but, seeing me at this lark, she very sensibly ruled against it.

Just then Danny arrived with one shoe on and the other off. He slumped down beside my father on the soft seat and joined in with the singing. I struggled across to buy him a drink and to ask him to keep an eye open for the hyena. I trod on his toe when I came back with his pint and he nearly sobered up with the pain.

Later on I did get a chance to identify the hyena, but I was in no position to exploit it. I was down in the toilet getting sick all over my shoes. I saw his shadow, felt him slap my back and heard him tell me to get it up out of me, heard him snigger and whinny his way up the stairs and accelerate into a side-splitting shriek that sent the whole bar above me reeling into fits of laughter.

Crunch lay on his old dishevelled bed with the sound of the Angelus chiming across the frost bound rooftops. His nerve-ends were all a tingle and his mouth felt like the inside of an old boot and the clamour that floated up from the street sent a piercing pain right through him. He sat up in bed, as haggard as a scarecrow, and reached across to the lopsided locker where his Sweet Afton cigarettes and matches were thrown. He lit up and coughed, exhaling a ring of smoke that hovered like a cloud and then snaked its way towards the brown-stained ceiling.

It was a damp gloomy room, sparsely fitted with ancient ugly furniture and dull torn wallpaper that drooped and bowed, having come away from the wall in places. There was a china sink in the corner and a bare, dust-speckled bulb hanging down. Covering the floor was a maggoty old carpet that was soggy with condensation, and overall there was a sour fragrance that Crunch, to his secret shame, seemed to have grown accustomed to.

The bells continued to clang, a fairly discordant jangle by anyone's standards, and suddenly it dawned on him that it was Christmas Eve. Come to think of it the bells rang all day yesterday too, presumably to remind him that it was the day before Christmas Eve. He had a vision of some mad bell ringer, or a mob of them perhaps, swinging fearlessly from the ropes above in the raftered belfry.

Crunch threw back the covers with an angry moan and stepped across to the wash-hand basin where he spluttered and splashed himself awake, coming up nice and easy from the sink to gaze into the jagged piece of snapped off mirror that was jammed between the splintered doorjamb and the door. And there he was, his downhearted double - a sick, wrecked Lazarus with bleared bloodshot eyes and a lived-in face and a slept-in shirt and his hair tossed up in a comical fashion; his teeth were bad and his lips were chapped and the stubble around his chin was turning grey and the veins around his eyes were blue and broken.

'Aw every day is Christmas if you've the money,' he heard himself mutter as he turned off the tap. 'Every day's the same!'

Crunch put on his pants, searching the pockets in vain. In his stockinged feet he padded out to the communal lavatory on the lower landing where it flowed out of him like the Horse River. Those living below heard (and griped about) his deep groan of manly satisfaction. Now he recognised the tune. It was his favourite hymn:

Hail Queen of heaven
The Ocean Star
Guide of the wanderer here below
Thrown on life's surge
We claim thy care
Save us from peril
And from woe
Mother of Christ
Star of the sea
Pray for the wanderer
Pray for me.

He tossed his smoked fag into the bowl and flushed it out of sight. He was surely a lost wandering soul and that hymn must have been written especially with him in mind. Suddenly he was thinking about things that had absolutely nothing whatsoever to do with the way he felt: when he was a boy and used to go out hunting with his ferret stuck up his jumper; or coming home from a hurling match down a darkening road with a crowd of hardy lads, all jeering and pucking one another. Or the time they robbed the orchard at the back of the nursery. Of course a few apples wouldn't do him. No, he had to go and rob a huge sackful and himself and Farrell were hard set to carry it home between them. If they had been caught that night it would have been six months in Artane or someplace for the pair of them. Poor old Toby Farrell, eh? - that sly little thief in the night!

Back in his room he went to the window and pulled aside the smoke-stained curtains to look out on a sea of slated roofs and dirty chimneys that went slanting all the way down to the waterfront. They say that you can tell the state of a man's life by taking in the view from his back door. Well, right now his didn't look too rosy - a clumsy junkyard with broken-down jalopies and rusty scrap iron strewn all about; tyres and wheels and pipes tossed into the long grass and the stripped remains of an old outmoded plough hidden in the weeds; cats perched and pissing on ugly walls, and a white-walled forgotten graveyard that was truly overgrown and tangled up with thorns and briars.

He came away from the window and sat down on the side of the bed, pulling his shoes out from under it with his foot. Manoeuvring to the edge he stooped to fasten his laces, grunting and growling like some old toothless codger. In one of his shoes he discovered a handful of small change and a crinkled-up pound note, and on the bedside locker he spied ten bob hidden behind the upended clock, and suddenly there was a great splash of hope surging through him, suddenly the hymn didn't seem so forlorn after all.

> *Mother of Christ*
> *Star of the sea*
> *Pray for the wanderer*
> *Pray for me.*

Yes, every day is Christmas if you've the money.

&

Johnny combed his hair and parted it to perfection. He thumbed his way through the array of suits that were hanging in the wardrobe. Laid out on the bed were his white starched shirt and an elegant bow tie and a new pair of socks, still sporting the label. He picked the striped suit, brushing it down and draping it across the back of the chair. Downstairs a radio played and the sound from the neighbourhood below had an odd, otherworldly ring to it: the disembodied voices of children playing Queeny-I-O on the footpath and the roar and rumble of a few teenagers working on a crock of a car, revving the engine and banging doors.

He turned the alarm clock around to check the time and as he dressed he went through the pattern the rest of the day would take - first off a stroll along the Quay, dropping off a pair of mended brogues on the way, then a feed in the Small Hotel followed by a few drinks in the bar there; after that it was into The Shamrock for a bit of a Christmas stave with Paddy and the boys.

Johnny was dressed now, all barring his shoes, which still needed a bit of a rub. He toddled downstairs with them and rummaged in the cardboard box under the sink for a brush, polish and an old rag. *The Green Green Grass Of Home* was on the radio and Johnny caught himself unconsciously moving to the beat of the song. When the shoes were shining he slipped them on and went back upstairs again to fetch a clean handkerchief from the small drawer beside the bed and to splash on some aftershave. He gave himself the once-over in the wardrobe mirror, turning sideways to flick a speck of dandruff from his shoulder.

Downstairs he turned off the radio, checked the back door, took his key from the nail, scooped up whatever loose change was on the table and headed down the hall, doubling back for the parcel of mended shoes he'd forgotten.

'*It's Good To Touch...*' he twittered as he blessed himself going out the door, and when he was gone the empty place, as if missing him, sighed and creaked and groaned: the cistern grumbled, the pictures frowned, the tap in the kitchen dripped and the various clocks ticked and tocked throughout the house as the rest of the furniture sulked in the shadows and hid from the waning light.

It was a fine fresh day outside with a healthy nip in the air as Johnny ambled down the street, smiling at this one, calling across the road to that one, and all the while still whistling his own ornate version of *The Green Green Grass Of Home.* Here it must be stated that Johnny had one of those happy walks that could brighten up the dreariest day. It had rhythm, style, panache. It very nearly had a melody, and of course like most happy things it was laced with sadness. Sometimes after Johnny had said hello to you and gone on by you felt something stirring inside you, some strange tender yearning, like you wanted to cry or something, and, try all you want, but you'd never know why.

Tweet tweet tweet tweet tweet tweet tweet...

Johnny dropped the mended shoes off at a house in Lower King Street and before he knew it he was on the Quay, mingling with all the other lovely living things, blending into the picture so perfectly. His walk became just another motion, his whistle was merely another sound, and soon he was just a speck, a stain, a painter's dab you might say on the sad, serrated soul of the universe. And if you look at it that way then I suppose what difference could it possibly make one way or another to anyone that this just happened to be his last sweet day under heaven. *Tweet tweet tweet tweet tweet tweet tweet tweet tweet tweet.*

𝄢

Mary heard the heavy footsteps crunch up the noisy, gravelled path and she knew straight away it was him. Her heart began to flutter at the thought of seeing him again, but she contrived to keep her face frosty and indifferent as only a hard-headed woman in love can do.

When Hickey's bulky body shaded the doorway his green guilty eyes avoided looking directly into hers. He stepped inside, loitering and mooning like a shy cowboy in the pictures. She was delighted to see him so mournful. 'Oh, did you come back?' she sort of sang, and the frankness in her voice made him look even more ill at ease.

Mary continued to wring out the wet cardigan in the sink, mumbling something about there being a cup of tea in the pot if he wanted one. He shambled across and helped himself, searching for the sugar in vain (everything had been changed around), and in the end, for handiness sake, going without. She wanted to run to him and melt in his arms, she wanted to tell him that she was glad to see him again, but of course she didn't. No, she carried on twisting and screwing that stupid wet cardigan dry instead as if it was the be-all and end-all of everything.

'Sit down before you fall down,' she chided as she slipped out to the washing line.

He obeyed and when she heard the scrape of the chair, in spite of it all, she managed a smile.

Out at the clothesline she pegged the dripping cardigan upside down and watched it dangle. Like a trapeze artist's pelt it swung there in the wind, buttons spinning, arms flapping helplessly, as empty and heartless and hopeless as they come. But she still couldn't bring herself to look over her shoulder at the kitchen window where he was bound to be sitting, anxiously watching and waiting. Looking anywhere but there - at the village, bleak and desolate now; at the beach where wave after thunderous wave fell and weltered against the kelp-strangled piling; at the vast, open ocean curving off to the other side of the world.

The wind blew back her hair, exposing her ears to the elements and whooshing her dress in close against her legs. She looked at her hands: red and hard from housework, fingers all tobacco stained and her nails nervously bitten to the quick; her nose ran with the cold too and when she reached inside her sleeve for a tissue she discovered it was no longer there so that she had to discreetly use the back of her hand. The whole universe seemed to be mocking her now, warning her that it was far too late in the day for all of this, that she was too old and long in the tooth to feel this way. *Mary Meek And Mary Mild*, she murmured as she turned and headed back towards the house again, catching a peripheral glimpse of him in the window.

Back inside the kitchen she noticed that Hickey had not slipped his bag in its usual convenient place close to the door, but on top of the built-in wardrobe in a definite, permanent sort of way.

'Did you miss me?' he grinned cheekily, his round face on fire from walking against the wind and his hair tossed and unruly.

'Yes, I did,' she replied, much to his surprise.

&

Earlier that morning Paddy Wolfe had coughed his way downtown. He moved, with an old prize-fighter's bouncing gait, past the unopened shops as they prepared for the busy day - the messenger boys dismantling the shutters and arranging the first load of parcels on their heavy bicycles, the sturdy butchers lugging in sides of meat, queues of shop girls waiting outside to be let in and pernickety managers jangling keys with that unctuous air of self-importance; groups of sad-faced, hung-over men too, moping about from corner to corner in the hope that they might soon get in somewhere.

Paddy knew that Davy was behind him. If he slowed up or stopped they could have walked down together. But he didn't, and the boy didn't run to catch up with him. They walked, a stone's throwaway from each other, father and son, down Rowe Street and onto Main Street, past the shops and bars and the grey Protestant chapel, into the Bull Ring and past the fish market, onto the Quay, where Paddy joined forces with George. The two men discussed what lay ahead of them, sighing and commiserating with one another and each pledging allegiance to the other as they went their separate ways. When Paddy eventually hauled out the keys of The Shamrock Davy conveniently stepped right up behind him and followed him in without further ado.

Soon Paddy was on the phone for some last minute ordering while Davy got straight into stocking up the shelves. Up and down the stairs he went, carrying two crates at a time, muttering and mumbling and taking notes, trying to cover every conceivable catastrophe, leaving spare crates of beer and porter just inside the cellar door and out of sight on the top landing, and bottles of whisky and gin in boxes concealed underneath the bench in the snug.

Up in the lounge a fire had to be lit, and the stairs needed mopping down. Paddy took care of all that while Davy slipped out to the bank and picked up a few dozen new tumblers in Barkers on his way back. These glasses had to be washed and stacked and barrels of draught porter and ale and lager had to be rolled in from the yard and the Gents had to be hosed down and the Ladies had to be seen to. Then, as Paddy began sorting out the till, counting out a float and that sort of thing, Davy fixed the tables into place and distributed the ashtrays and beer mats.

At half past ten on the dot the door was flung open and pinned back and the blind on the front window was released. A finger of wintry sunlight invaded the snug, falling across the tail end of the counter and dappling the tiny shelves that held the ginger ale and the runty bottles of tonic water; and when Davy opened the overhead window the metallic to-do from the street (the clang of the window cleaner's bucket and the scrape of his ladder and the clopping dray going by) was suddenly distinct and clearly identifiable.

℔

The first time the bell rang upstairs I was as composed as a hotel night porter. I went up and served the two old ladies their Harvey's Bristol Cream Sherries and leisurely put more fuel on the fire before coming back down again. But in the few minutes I was away all sense of order had left the bar. The place had suddenly filled up and the Guinness barrel was empty and I had already run out of small bottles of lager. I tried to pacify the newcomers, dashing down to the cellar between orders. Through the magic door I spied the outline of another few old women traipsing upstairs for their Christmas drink. Soon the bell was ringing again and when I got the chance I hurried up there to see what they wanted as my father took up his position on the soft seat, starting off the day with *I'm Dreaming Of A White Christmas*. Very nice!

I was up and down those stairs by the new time that day, coming back to find Flash Harrys calling for drinks for the house, and drunks arguing and sometimes fighting. Before the morning was over I had on my hands one man crying, one man bleeding and a young lad throwing up all over the place. I had to clean it up, squeezing out through the crowd that were crammed together like passengers into the tiny snug.

Once I ran out of change and I had to rush into The Small Hotel to see if George had any to spare. He was up to his ears too and just as narky as I was. I returned to find that somebody had collapsed and spilt a rake of pints all over the floor. I cut my hand trying to clear up the mess and wasted more time trying to stop the bleeding. We had no plasters and I was forced to hurry back into The Small Hotel again to see if George could fix me up. On my return the fallen hero had come to and wanted me to call him a taxi. I told him to hang on and battled my way through the snug to get to the phone, only to hear the bell upstairs ringing as another fight brewed down by the dartboard. My father, who had been more or less oblivious to the problems up til then, realised that this was a serious row and one that I wouldn't be able to handle. He put down his accordion and threw the main culprit out, head first. George appeared and disappeared in a flash, put off by the rush.

My father performed in spasms, enticing the newcomers to join in, letting the really inebriated ones go and starting up again when the time was right. Some time in the afternoon my mother turned up to lend a hand and between the two of us we managed to get the place back into some semblance of order again, but no sooner were we finished than the whole thing started up once more and by seven o'clock in the evening the place was as bad as it ever was.

We took it in turns to slip out for a cup of tea. I went up to Forte's Café on the corner, bumping into Kathy on the way. I faked a casual smile and lost myself in the crowd as the sound of her voice lanced me to the quick. I sat at a table by the window and tried to forget the shape of her face. Danny, who was passing by outside, spotted me and came in to see how I was doing.

'Hey, I see your old flame on the town,' he said. 'Did you see her?'

I pretended I hadn't.

'She looks deadly, boy,' he continued. 'She has these pair of tight jeans on her. She has a grand arse.'

I expect Danny thought it was alright to talk like that about her now that she was no longer going out with me, and I suppose in a way it was. I bought him a cup of tea and let him have half my sandwich. He said that it was a pity I had to work, that the town was crawling with young ones. He had his mod suit on and his hair was covered in Christmas frost. When the little Casey one passed by the cafe Danny's eyes lit up and he clapped his hands together and winked at me as if he was going to tackle her that very night.

Back at The Shamrock my mother was sweeping another broken glass off the floor and sighing, 'God, will this day ever be done,

Davy.'

There was no music now. My father was in at the sink, washing glasses. The minute I showed my face behind the counter I was inundated with orders.

'What's the matter with Johnny?' my mother wondered as she lifted the counter flap.

'I don't know,' I said, going about my work.

'He's not himself at all,' she said.

'Look, don't worry about him,' I said, and asked her to put on a few pints of stout for me.

I was too busy to worry about anybody right then and so I hardly gave Johnny a second thought. But there was something strange about the way he was carrying on that night. There was a wild, hunted look about him with his hair tossed drunkenly and drink spilt uncharacteristically down the front of his shirt. And he was totally unreasonable, ordering treble whiskies and trying to drink them raw and asking me to top it up again before his glass was even half-empty. In the end I was topping it up with lemonade and he never even copped it.

At the end of the night we were all numb and stupefied and more than a little relieved that the day was over. All around us bodies were being led and carried out to taxis and cars, and the walking wounded helped one another to the door. My father was prowling, shepherding them all out into the night. He became annoyed as he watched a few stragglers dawdling behind, some of them wanting carry-outs and packets of cigarettes.

'Aw, come on lads, it's well after time,' he called out like a auctioneer.

'Stop the noise, Paddy,' Hickey slurred, stuffing a bottle of scotch in one pocket and a naggin of vodka into the other.

Joe Crofton was helping Johnny to his feet, putting one arm (like a ventriloquist's dummy) around his waist and swinging one of Johnny's arms over his shoulder.

'What about Rip Van Winkle?' my father said to him, meaning Forty Winks who was dead to the world on the counter.

'What's that?' Joe Crofton said, propping Johnny for a few seconds up against the wall to give the matter some thought. 'Oh, just point him in the right direction, Paddy. He's able to sleepwalk his way home at this stage.'

My father made an attempt to smile, throwing his eyes to heaven as another drunken '*jowlster*' shook his hand and wished him a happy Christmas. George reappeared, looking knackered, and eyed the smoky ruin of The Shamrock which looked like the aftermath of a circus now: the place layered with broken bottles, fag ends, overturned ashtrays, empty cigarette packets, dribbling kicked-over bottles of stout, racing dockets and scraps of newspaper that had been shredded and scattered and strewn.

'Give George a glass of Jameson there, Davy,' my father said as he closed the door on the last staggering straggler.

'No, Paddy, I haven't cleared the place yet. There are still a couple of boyos propping one another up in there,' George said. 'A bottle of stout, Davy... I'll be back after.'

'That was rough, George,' I said as I poured out his Guinness.

'What would you know about it?' George jested and lowered his welcome drink with relish, adding as he vanished, 'I'll give you a tap on the window.'

⚓

Johnny was found dead on Christmas morning. He suffocated in his sleep. Joe Crofton said that he probably felt sick in the night and couldn't get himself up out of the bed. I kept thinking about the impressive pile of money that Johnny had left behind him on the counter. I had scooped it up and dropped it into a handled jug, thinking how delighted Johnny would be when he came into the bar on St Stephen's Day to discover that he had an unexpected nest egg stashed away.

We buried him on a cold, bleak day. The funeral procession stopped for a few minutes outside the Shoebox and, as we moved along, the burning question seemed to be what was going to become of his shop now that Johnny was gone. Some old man behind me, who seemed to know all the ins and outs of the matter, informed us that the place actually belonged to Ned Stand, that Johnny was only renting it from him. Hickey told us all then that he heard that Ned Stand intended to set his big fat wastrel son up in business there now, and everyone seemed to agree that Ned Stand's son was nothing only a big waster.

As we treacled down onto the Quay the fishermen stopped working, took off their hats and caps and blessed themselves, some of them falling in alongside us. Behind them Useless Island seemed to sink downhearted into the sea and as we crossed the bridge I glanced back for a last look at The Shamrock. My mother was upstairs in the lounge, looking out at the funeral, and there were a few distant figures huddled together under the canopy of The Small Hotel.

Before I knew it the whole thing was over and we were trudging down the stony aisles of the cemetery, breaking up into various groups to discuss the plan. Men in working clothes made their way towards the gate to grab their lifts back into town. They would head for the nearest pub for a quick one before dashing red-faced back to work. I dawdled down the avenue, reading the many tombstones as I passed: Delaney and Dempsey and Whelan and all the other Wexford men and women who have been laid to rest here. Some of the graves were majestic with big ornate tombstones and winged angels and white urns for flowers and black and white fancy stones that sparkled like jewels. Other graves looked sad and neglected with no tombstone at all, just a rusty old cross to mark the spot. I was feeling kind of mixed up to say the least - sad, angry, confused, take your pick. I had been at funerals before, mainly relatives - aunts and uncles and grannies for the most part - but this was different. Johnny had come into my life a stranger. I was not compelled to love him or to feel sorry at his death. He had earned my love. He had wooed and won my respect, the same as Mickey Fury had done all those years ago. And now the terrible finality of it all was brought home to me: Mickey Fury would not be coming back; he would not turn up out of the blue someday, bronzed and bearded; he did not swim ashore to some primitive island when his ship went down off the coast of Galatz.

'Here son, do you want a lift?' someone called out to me.

'Yeah, thanks very much,' I said and hurried over to the car.

'Get in the back there,' the driver said, getting out his side to let me in.

'Have you room?' I wondered, looking in at the other men who were crowded together in the back.

'Oh, I dare say we'll squeeze you in alright. Sure you're not that big or anything,' the driver said, ushering me into the car.

'How are you young Wolfe,' this oily man said as I climbed in beside him.

'Well thanks,' I said and acknowledged the rest of the men.

'How's your da?' the oily man quizzed, lighting up a cigarette and lowering the window to toss the spent match out.

'He's in right form. He was out there in the graveyard today-somewhere,' I said, looking out the window to see if I could see him anywhere.

'Was he? I never laid eyes on him.'

'All over bar the shoutin' now, lads' the driver said, banging his door shut and starting up the car. 'He had a great turnout all the same.'

'Oh yeah,' the oily man agreed. 'Aw, Johnny was a grand fella,' and everyone agreed that Johnny was a grand fellow.

The avenue to the cemetery was chock-a-block with people and cars, all trying to get out. Victor was there, beckoning our car on with one hand, controlling the crowd with the other.

'Good man Victor. No bother to you, boy,' the driver shouted out the open window as we drove past. 'What would we do without him, lads?'

'Who's that? Oh, Victor ... A harmless poor aul'divil too,' the oily man said as we drove out onto the road.

'Where's everybody gettin' out now?' the driver wanted to know as we drove past Kaat's Strand.

'Drop us off at the end of the bridge anyway,' the oily man said, meaning himself and the quiet chap in the front. 'We've to go back to work, back to the grind. Some of us have to work, ain't that right, Tony?'

'That's right,' Tony in the front said.

'Are you not goin' for a pint?' the driver wondered.

'No, I am not. This is our second funeral this week. The queer fella nearly had a heart attack when we told him we were going to another one this mornin'.'

'Where are ye workin' anyway, lads?'

'Over in Halligan's there.'

'Oh, the garage is it?'

'Yeah.'

'Halligan. Hooligan we call him. Jaysus he's an awful looking sketch altogether, ain't he?' the driver was saying as the bridge came into view.

'Yeah. And his brother is worse. Big mad looking eyes and hairy eyebrows on him,' the oily man said. 'Do you know him?'

'What? Oh, yes I do. You wouldn't want to bump into that lad on a dark night. He'd frighten the shite out of you, that's all. Do not feed while performing, hah?'

'Oh stop.'

'Every hair on his back is rank poison...'

'The only two of their kind in captivity,' Tony in front, already red at the gills, shyly drawled.

'Good man, Tony,' the oily man laughed.

And on and on it went like that until we pulled in at the end of the bridge and it began to rain, little needles of rain that drummed on the roof and trickled down the windscreen.

'Here's the rain,' the driver said, turning on the wipers.

'Yeah, even the angels are cryin', lads,' the oily man declared as they clambered out of the car.

'Don't work too hard now, boys,' the driver called after them as the three men darted across the road. 'Give my regards to the Missing Link.'

'I might as well get out here too,' I said.

'What? Sure, I'm goin' up to The Shamrock anyway.'

'The Shamrock is closed this morning.'

'Well, where's all the boys goin' then - your da and all?'

'The Small Hotel, I think.'

'What? Oh, I'll let you out here so. I'm not mad about that place at all. There's a queer aul' snobby aul' clique gets in there. Tell your da I'll see him durin' the week.'

'Right,' I promised, even though I didn't know the man from Adam, and then I took myself off up the Quay and into the bar of The Small Hotel, where George wondered with a glance what I was drinking. I ordered a pint of ale and sat up at the bar beside Forty Winks, who signalled to George that he'd pay for it.

'Thanks Timmy,' I said as I waited.

'You're welcome, Davy,' a broken-hearted looking Forty Winks replied.

'He had a fair funeral,' George said when he served me.

'Yeah, he surely did. Were you out there?'

'No. I only went as far as the end of the bridge, that's all. We've a wedding here this morning, so I had to get back. A fairly big do it is too.'

'You'll be kept goin' so,' I commiserated, glancing over my shoulder. 'I'd say the boys are into it for the day.'

'Oh, yes they are,' George said and wiped the counter, gingerly. 'Here's the boss now.'

My father came in stomping and cheerful as if nothing was up, but his eyes were moist with sadness. He called for a drink for the house, plonking himself down beside Joe Crofton and peeling off a twenty spot from a wad of notes.

'Here y'are young fella, get that into you,' George said, planting my second pint up in front of me.

'Don't leave Junior out anyway,' my father bellowed across the bar and everybody laughed with relief.

'That'll put hairs on your chest, Davy,' Forty Winks commented sadly as he rose and nipped into the toilet.

Just then a real straight-backed gentleman came in, followed by a lady with a silly hat and white gloves. She sat cross-legged in front of the fire, showing the top of her stocking to anyone who happened to be sitting at the right angle (which most of us were at that time). The man ordered a large brandy and a dry sherry and was engaged in a long secretive confab with George about something or other.

Slowly but surely the cosy bar filled up and soon the place was buzzing as if nothing was ever amiss.

'If I had my way I'd shoot the lot of them,' this elderly chain-smoker was saying. He was referring to the men on the dole.

'Could you possibly hang on about a month or so,' Durango Clark begged, grinning. 'I've a bit of a tangle comin' up, then you can fire away.'

'No, be honest though, lads. There are lads down there and they wouldn't work in a fit. Never worked a day in their lives and don't bloody well want to work,' said your man crossly. He had a priestly pallor and looked like an executioner with a stoop that in the right light could easily pass for a hump.

'That's true enough right enough,' someone else agreed and my father coughed and said, 'Bloody jowlsters, the lot of them!'

'There's a guy is doin' queer well for himself,' Durango said, changing the subject and digging into his pocket.

'Who's that?'

'How much do you want, George?'

'Twelve bob, Durango.'

'Twelve bob. There's ten and two for yourself. Thank you sir.'

'Thanks,' George said, scooping up the money coin by finger-flicked coin.

'That Lacy chap,' Durango continued. 'I believe he's after buyin' The Hole In The Wall.'

'I heard it's up for sale alright,' my father said, more or less verifying the rumour.

'I heard he's goin' to modernise it and everything,' Durango revealed with a clever wink. 'New toilets, lounge, the lot.'

'That's not the lad that sells the papers is it?' Joe Crofton inquired.

'No, that's Eddie. This other fella would be a brother of Eddie's. Eddie wouldn't have tuppence to rub together.'

'A great yodely voice on him?' someone said.

'Yeah, Eddie. He wouldn't have that kind of money.'

'I don't know about that,' Joe Crofton interjected. 'I bought a paper off him last Sunday and he did well out of it anyway. I gave him a pound note and he only gave me change of ten bob. I never noticed it until I was half way home. My last pound too,' Joe Crofton complained.

'That's right, he has a great yodel in his voice alright,' my father said, and demonstrated with a wild shriek, '*H-e-a-r-l-d-a-P-r-e-s-s.* He reminds me of your man on the radio. Whats-his-name ... Billy Cotton ... *Wakey wakey key* ....'

'Sure they calls him Slim Whitman, don't they,' Durango reminded everyone.

'I'm not fuckin' surprised,' Joe Crofton said sourly. 'Ten and thrupence for an Independent. I'd say he has as much money as Slim Whitman too, accordin' to that.'

The wedding party was eventually called down to the dining room for the meal. The tousle-headed bellboy went around ringing a bell and calling out, 'Will all the people attending the O'Brien-Murphy wedding please take their seats in the dining-room.' He shouted that out a few times, then responded to George's mimed command to collect some empty glasses. Soon there was a great exodus from the bar as all the wedding guests trooped downstairs for their meal and most of the funeral-goers went back to work or into The Shamrock, which was now open for business. George was weary from all the running around and treated himself to a well earned rest in the corner with a quiet cup of tea while I sat alone, staring drunkenly into my pint.

'What's up?' Joe Crofton said, stepping right up beside me.

I looked up at him and I knew that he knew. And I told him so. I told him about the money in the jug and not knowing what to do with it and I said that some of us, his so-called friends, should have stopped him, somebody should have asked him what was up. Joe Crofton turned away from me, wincing as if he knew what was wrong with Johnny all along but couldn't tell me, couldn't tell anyone.

'Give us another drink here, George,' he said.

I waved him away, indicating that I had enough.

'Go on, have one more. It won't kill you,' he said, giving George the bend to pull me another pint.

'No, I think he has enough,' George decided, looking me over.

Joe Crofton pressed no further with it, ordered another drink for himself and Forty Winks and then turned to me with merciful eyes.

'Look, take whatever money is in it and get yourself a few strings for your guitar or somethin',' he said. 'Or if you don't want to do that, go up to the chapel and buy a couple of mass cards.' He stopped then and sort of sighed and brushed his falling down hair away from his face, 'Because Johnny was one sound man, Davy... One sound man, boy!'

I silently agreed. Forty Winks did too with a comforting hand on my shoulder. I tried to remain calm, I really did, but in the end I broke down and Forty Winks tried to console me, crying himself inside I expect, as the rain scratched and tapped against the rattling hotel window.

CHAPTER EIGHT

I stood outside the closed up dancehall and watched the rheumy-eyed caretaker place the sign (upside down at first) in the glass, panelled box. He stood back to admire his handiwork before returning inside to turn out the lights. I stooped to read the writing even though I knew well enough what was scribbled there. Last night was New Year's Eve and the last frenzied ejaculation of the Christmas season. Last night I had danced to The Miami Showband, heard Fran O'Toole singing *Semi-Detached Suburban Mister James*, kissed a perfect stranger a Happy New Year and saw Kathy clinging to someone else, dancing around with her eyes closed, and there was no doubt in my mind that from here on out it was all downhill.

This happened every year at this time and I never got used to the sting of it as that handwritten sign plunged us all, like it or not, into the very heart of the gloomy winter. I stood there in the cold, reading

the message over and over again. The wet road gleamed with rai
reflecting the neon signs and shop lights all the way up the narrc
street. I was probably there too if you looked real close, immured in
puddle, lodged between Holly's Toy Shop and O'Brien's chipper. Ar
something told me I should make a run for it before this small tow
boy became a small town man.

Then the caretaker came out and banged shut the heavy door c
the hall which gave back its empty echo. He checked the door wit
the weight of his body, shot me a wary glance, grumbled and wad
dled homeward. I snapped out of my trance and moved along as well
aimlessly. Danny would be up in the Boker Poker Club, but I didn'
really fancy listening to Skeleton Delaney tonight. Nolan's Cafe was
finished for me too. I'd be eighteen in ten days and it was time to be
moving on. It was a pity, but that's the way I felt. I'd miss the jukebox
of course (*Reach Out* by The Four Tops had just been installed and
Bobby Darin singing Tim Hardin's song *If I Was A Carpenter*) and
I'd miss all the lovely girls that went in and out of there too, gloves
and cigarettes on the table, sipping their cokes and nibbling their ice
cream sundaes.

I would have plenty of time off for the next few months and no
where to go. My father would be as moody as hell, not plotting an
scheming how to save his business any more but resigned to losing tl
whole shebang. My mother would do her best to humour him wh
I'd stay out of the way altogether for fear I'd bear the brunt of it all

I decided to buy a bag of chips and go on home, go up to my roi
and practise my guitar, try to figure out how to play *My Girl*, annoy
heart and soul out of the neighbours. As I walked up the near dese
Main Street I caught a brief glimpse of myself in a shop winc
My hair was all frizzled, tossed and blown about with the wind
the rain, and my 'bum freezer' overcoat looked kind of corny. !
my Beatle boots looked out of style. My face looked real ordin:
felt real ordinary. It certainly didn't look like the face of a blok
was going to travel the world and come back rich and famou
tattooed and cocksure of himself, but still the same old Davy W
the back of it all. No, it just looked like plain old Davy Wolfe

Davy Wolfe who was going nowhere fast, who was never meant to go anywhere, who would walk up and down this one horse town until he was blue in the face, who might stop once in a while to look up at and wonder about and maybe even listen to the stars.

'How are you, Davy? How is your mammy keeping?'

'Grand.'

'How's your da?'

'He's in great form, thanks.'

'Who's that chap?'

'That's young Davy Wolfe: Paddy's young lad.'

'God, I didn't know him. He's after getting tall.'

The two permed, elderly women disappeared into Rowe Street chapel yard. As she went the one that didn't recognise me glanced back at me and serenely smiled. The two of us are bound together somehow. She was there when I got my hand caught in the spokes of the bicycle; she witnessed Mickey Fury trying to hug away the fright and the pain. She saw him trying to push the clock back those few awful seconds, and then she picked up the severed joint and placed it in a handkerchief. She told me years later that she had buried it in her back garden, that it had grown into a beautiful blood-red rose. She said it got bigger and more beautiful every year. I never saw it, but whenever I try to picture it it's always a strong looking flower with a majestic stem. It has a full voluptuous body that constantly sheds and scatters reams and reams of petals symmetrically around her garden. Sometimes there are drops of blood dripping from it, staining the grass and the cement path that lead to her clothesline. Sometimes they are not drops of blood but tiny silver tears that fall with a splash to wash away the stains. There is always a spacious glasshouse in the background and an apple tree weighed down with fruit and a whitewashed stable full of straw. I realise this is impossible since her garden, like ours, is just a cluttered backyard. My mother is always there somewhere too. I can't see her or anything, just sort of sense her standing in the wings, beside me or behind me somewhere.

The two old women were out of sight now, probably in the chapel blessing themselves with holy water from the font inside the door. I

never asked her to let me see the rose. I don't suppose I ever will now. Wouldn't it be great if her story was true?

ȷ

It was Ash Wednesday, the beginning of Lent, and there was an eerie stillness about the town. Every man in the place was abstaining from something or other - drinking, smoking or cursing. Business in The Shamrock was abysmal. I was going without wages and every-thing. Most days there was nothing for me to do. On top of Lent there was also a mission on in town, which put the kybosh on the idea that some of the lads might relent after a couple of days.

Two sinister black figures had gunslinged their way into town about a month ago, coming back from the heart of the jungle where it was said they had converted a couple of thousand Mau Maus. One was an old fellow with a reassuring face. The other was a young man with a pale complexion, soft delicate hands and a pair of gold-rimmed spectacles. He looked like a member of the Gestapo, stern and un-shakable. He was the one who had gone out into the Dairy Fields and hunted the courting couples out of the long grass, giving the boys an earful and driving the girls in front of him like a herd of brazen hussies. He threatened too to go into any bar that had its doors open while the men's retreat was on. He claimed the right to do this by reminding everybody that Jesus had not been afraid to bullwhip the greedy merchants and thieves out of the temple. He pointed out that he would be doing the very same thing only in reverse.

I had made up my mind not to attend the mission this year. And as I walked down the empty Main Street with my dirty cross of blessed ashes on my forehead I stuck to the shadows, afraid that any minute one of those missioners would pounce out of a side street and nab me. All the bars and shops were closed. Now and again a few sly looking chancers would step out of some louche laneway and tap on a side door or window, acting nonchalant until I went on by. I was trying to get to the Boker Poker Club where I would do the very same thing - tap on the window three times and shout my name in through the letterbox.

That was the night I first met and spoke to the little Casey one, the girl that was supposed to have given Skeleton Delaney all he wanted behind the gasworks yard. She just came across the street to me and, with a kind of embarrassed expression, asked me if she could walk along with me awhile. She said that there was this drunken man up in front and he had said something to her. She was afraid of him. That man turned out to be Dancer. We crossed over onto the other footpath when we came close to him. He didn't say anything. He just looked our way and blew some snot from his nose, blocking one nostril with his finger. The little Casey one shuddered as we passed him, gripping my elbow with her frightened hands. I said that I would walk her all the way home, that I was in no real hurry at all. She seemed relieved. We talked about real ordinary things: our blessed ashes and what we gave up for lent and that. Then she told me that she knew my sister and I said that I had gone to school with her brother, Paul, and wondered where he was. He was working in England now, she said, adding that she was really surprised to discover she actually missed him. She seemed like a real nice girl to me.

'Well, how did you get on?' Danny beamed when I finally got to the Boker Poker Club.

It seems I was clocked with the little Casey one and everyone assumed that I had shifted her. I tried to explain that I was just walking along with her because she was afraid, that there was nothing in it.

'Did you even try her?' Danny asked me.

'No,' I admitted.

'She asked you to walk her home and you didn't even try her?' Skeleton Delaney butted in.

'She asked me to walk that way with her because she was afraid, that's all,' I said, hoping that would put an end to the matter.

'What was she supposed to be afraid of?' Skeleton Delaney wondered.

I hesitated. I couldn't tell them that she was afraid of Dancer because he was a big noise in the Boker Poker Club.

'I don't know,' I said. 'The dark, I suppose.'

'Yeah, right,' Skelton Delaney sneered. 'Hey lads, come out here and hear this. What would you think of a lad not tryin' a bit of stuff who was so bullin' for it that she actually asked him to walk her home? Actually asked him now, mind! What would you say if I was to tell you that that fella didn't even tackle her?'

A few older men had arrived out of the back room- Yul Bryne and another swarthy looking individual - to hear the yarn. 'I'd say he was a queer,' one of them said.

I tried to point out to them that there was a big difference between shifting a girl from a dance or somewhere and in walking along with her because she was frightened. I said that it wouldn't matter what anyone said about her, it would be wrong to try anything like that if she just wanted you to walk a bit of the way with her because she was afraid. They were all amused at this train of thought. Most of them seemed to agree that if a girl was up for it then it was a fellow's duty to get on with it.

I was as red as beetroot now. Everyone was laughing at me, or so it seemed anyway. I was angry and embarrassed and so confused that I didn't know what to say or do. I was sitting down one minute and standing up the next and then walking around in circles. Why hadn't I gone to the fucking mission anyway? If I had gone this wouldn't be happening to me now. I wouldn't have met the little Casey one in the first place. I would have come down here as usual and no one would have even put any pass on me.

Danny got fed up of all the talk and stood up for me. 'Hey Skeleton, how do we know that what you say about the girl is true anyway?' he said. 'I mean we only have your word for that.'

'Yeah well, what's wrong with that?' Skeleton Delaney challenged him.

'Nobody ever saw you with her or anything,' Danny pointed out. 'As a matter of fact I don't think I ever saw you with a girl in my life. Maybe you're the queer, not Davy.'

Everybody laughed at this and Skeleton Delaney didn't like it at all.

Then two men who had been at the mission came in and everybody gathered round them to ask them what the sermon was about. Most of the fellows would let on to their wives or mothers that they were at it and they wanted to be able to tell them what the sermon was about. One of the men - a little balding boxer of a bloke - was elected to tell the story, verbatim by the sounds of it, while the other lad - a gawky, bushy haired chap with a tooth in the front missing and itching to get in on the act - interjected the odd scrap of information here and there. Anyway according to them the old priest was on duty and he was telling the congregation all about the time he was out in the heart of darkest Africa or somewhere, *a tiny island that was full of hungry souls.* Poor people, he said, who lived like peasants in ramshackle shacks not fit to put a dog in. These people took God into their hearts it seemed and they all got together and built a stone chapel that was dedicated to Our Lady Of Perpetual Succour.

'A white chapel,' the gawky fellow chipped it. 'On a hill.'

Anyway there was a rich white man on that island too who was as old as Methuselah. He was a decadent old Bwana who lived in a mansion and liked women and was always eating and drinking and had never done a hand's turn in his big fat life. This old geezer didn't have any time for the priest. He wouldn't even listen to him. He never came to the chapel or anything, not even at Christmas time when all these innocent peasants walked in a candlelit procession all around the island: at the front all the barefooted children marched, singing hymns and carols; all the women were next, covered up from head to toe (up to a few months before they all walked around stark naked, the other lad informed anyone who'd listen, well the few stragglers at the back of the gathering); all the men shuffled silently behind, bearing gifts - knives and bowls and shining silver pearls. It was this procession that made the old priest happier than he had ever been in his whole life. He was sure now that he had done his job. God was on the island and he could at last go back home to Ireland. (Here the gawky lad solemnly blessed himself as if the story was at an end and he made a little sobbing sound as it continued without him. 'Oh yeah,' he said under his breath.)

'Before he came home,' the narrator went on, 'the old priest decided that he would try one last time to get through to the old rich bastard.

He travelled up this swampy river in a makeshift boat, risked life and limb to get there too. All around him there were dangers – you know, snakes and crocodiles and poisonous plants and that. When he eventually arrived at the big house, cold and hungry and dead tired, he wasn't even offered so much as a glass of water. He pleaded with the old man for hours, begging him to listen and heed the things he had to say. But it was all in vain. The old man refused point-blank to mend his evil ways and the priest came away from there disappointed.'

'What could he do?' the gawky lad said, throwing his hands in the air.

'A fuckin' double act,' Yul Bryne grumbled.

'A few years later,' the bald fellow ploughed ahead, 'the same priest returned to that island and he was delighted at what he found. There was the big white chapel with a new bell tower standing on top of the hill and down in the valley there was a convent school where he heard a class of tiny brown children singing... *Dilin O Deamhas* or something.'

'What about the rich fella?' Yul Bryne pressed.

'I was comin' to that,' the storyteller said, stalling to light his cigarette from another man's scut and holding a '*forbidden to speak*' hand up at his comrade-in-arms.' ...and this is the best part,' he said.

His friend was nodding in the background. *Wait til you hear this,* he seemed to be saying.

'I'm afraid the rich man wasn't in too good shape, lads. In fact he was confined to a wheelchair, unable to - well barely able to anyway - move or talk or think, a blubbering, dribbling fool in fact.'

That was the general gist of the sermon anyway and the moral of the story seemed to be that when this old priest, or any priest for that matter, told you to change your life you'd better listen because God worked in wondrous ways.

Well, this smacked of voodoo to me and I said so. 'Voodoo,' I said and scoffed. I was the only one who thought it was amusing though, apart from Danny who eventually saw the humorous side of it and chuckled along with me. Everybody else was disgusted with us for behaving so sacrilegiously. Yul Bryne said that I mustn't be right in the head and they all scattered to various parts and corners of the club. I made myself laugh out loud then and Danny did too when he heard me taking off the hyena.

'Go away ye big queer,' the swarthy one called from the inner sanctum and a great cheer went up.

I got my coat and left the club, Danny following closely behind me, and we never went back there again.

&

The Shamrock emptied itself out onto the footpath as the parade went tramping by - the wailing pipe band with its giant leader twirling his big silver cane, the fife-and-drum band playing *Sean South from Garryowen*, the girl guides daintily filing past, the Boy Scouts in blue, the Foresters in green, The Knights Of Malta and the Legion Of Mary and The FCA followed by The Confraternity Brass and Reed Band and so on. And all the boys, half-drunk from a great morning's drinking, cheering whenever they spied someone they recognised. It made me sort of sad to watch them with their big sods of shamrock pinned awkwardly on to their good Sunday suits. In a roundabout way it put me in mind of Johnny, who always had a neat blob of shamrock hooked on to his lapel so that you could hardly see the pin or anything.

It also reminded me of when I was a boy and used to sit on the high windowsill in John Street to watch the Saint Patrick's Day parade go thundering by, fascinated by the coloured flags and the rumble of the drums. We used to time the parade to see how long it would take to pass our door, marvelling at the fact that when the start of the procession was going down Hill Street the back of it was only coming out of Rowe Street chapel yard. Then Mickey Fury and I would run along behind it, our Saint Patrick's Day badges flapping in the March breeze. In the afternoon there would be devotions in the chapel and we'd all sing *Hail Glorious Saint Patrick* and I'd think of poor Patrick alone on those dreary hills of Slane, minding the pigs, eating their swill and sleeping in a cold, dirty old shed. Then the bugle would ring out throughout the church, played by a big Boy Scout who we knew by sight, and we hoped and prayed that he wouldn't sound any duff notes and make a holy show of himself (and us for that matter) if there happened to be any Yanks in town to witness the event. He blew *The Last Post*, and it had such a lonely lost tone to it that it always kind of took the good out of the day for me.

Hickey caught sight of Lar Lyons marching past and pointed him out to us. Everyone cheered and jeered him as he went by. He was with the FCA (The Free Clothes Association was the running gag). 'Now we know where he got the boots, lads,' Durango Clark shouted, and Lar Lyons got so confused that he went out of step and had to give a brisk stylish hop and skip to fall back in time again. A great cheer went up at this and Hickey called out, 'Smile out of that Lyons and give your face a holiday.'

Over on the far side, standing on the Woodenworks, were Dancer and Easy Going Larry. Easy Going Larry seemed contented enough but the other fellow looked ill at ease to say the least. I turned away from him. I wasn't going to let him spoil the day on me. Nothing would do that now. Not even Kathy, who I'd seen earlier on waving to someone in the crowd. It was Saint Patrick's Day and everyone was automatically absolved from their Lenten vows. There would be drinking and singing and cursing to beat the band today, and tonight – thanks to a special dispensation – there would be a dance on in the Parish Hall. The Freshmen were coming down from the North, a band that could imitate the Beach Boys to a tee. Yes, tonight it would be *God Only Knows* and *Good Vibrations* and I bet Danny a pound to a penny that they'd do *Night Of Fear* by The Move.

I dawdled there outside until the entire parade had vanished around the bend and the last notes of the trumpets had blown away. The tinkling of the accordion inside began to drown the distant sounds of the fifes and the rumbling drums and soon the boys inside were singing *When Irish Eyes Are Smiling* and I roused myself and went back to work.

'Here he is now,' Hickey said as I came through the door.

'It's about time too,' someone else bellowed: Durango Clark I think it was.

'I thought you were after fuckin enlistin' or somethin',' Crunch ranted, beckoning for me to go in and pour him a drink before he *'expired'*.

⚓

That night I slipped upstairs to the old silent lounge where my good suit hung in a Marlowe's bag on the side of the piano. Downstairs a boisterous singsong was going on and I could hear the laughter and the dinging of the till as I slipped out of my working clothes. My mother had agreed to give me this busy night off provided I stocked up all the shelves and took care of everything in the cellar before I went. This was all done and, as I stood there in the half-light with the faulty neon sign outside squinting and the floorboards gently creaking, I thought of the cosy bar in The Small Hotel where Danny would be waiting for me, and I pictured the Parish Hall and the music that lay ahead. I felt fairly good as I stuffed the bundle of working clothes and shoes down behind the piano for safe keeping.

One last sideways look in the old **Guinness Is Good For You** looking glass before tramping downstairs for a glance at the bar just to make sure that everything was in order. My mother let me know that all was well and I caught a glimpse through the shamrock-shaped mirror of a bawdy scene that would haunt me forever more: Crunch was up in the corner singing *Malibar,* his raspy voice lilting from word to word as my father tried to accompanied him as best he could on the accordion; Joe Crofton was beside him, gazing pensively into his pint; Forty Winks was half asleep on the counter and Hickey was holding Mary's hand and grinning impishly. Only that afternoon she had stormed into the bar with a face of vengeance on her and plonked his black bag on the counter in front of him so that we all got the gist of the message. It seemed he never went home the night before and she was sick and tired of it all, and he was tugging at her sleeve, trying to get her to sit down and listen to his side of the story. I didn't give much for his chances to tell you the truth, but somehow or other he managed to worm his way back into her good books again, and here he was now holding her hand and winking at me to reassure me that

148

everything was back on track again.

Lar Lyons was still in his FCA uniform and acting like he had just got back from Vietnam. 'The Small Hotel must be on fire, lads,' he said as George slid past me and into the snug for a quick one, and I thought I heard George mumble, '*jowlster*' as I left.

Next door in The Small Hotel bar Danny, rejoicing at the sight of me, was sitting by the fire. We had a few pints there, and then we headed down to the dance, the two of us chuckling and joining in with the music hall medley that poured out of The Shamrock as we passed, Danny doing a nifty Bo Jangles shuffle out in the middle of the road:

> *When You're Smiling, When You're Smiling*
> *The Whole World Smiles With You*
> *When You're Laughing, Keep On Laughing....*

Over on the Woodenworks opposite I saw the sinister outline of Dancer sitting on a bollard, guzzling from a flagon of cider. He lit up a cigarette, the lighter glinting in the dark. Then he hocked and spat and sort of sneezed. 'Keep goin',' Danny said in my ear. 'Keep goin'...' he urged.

The dancehall foyer was in full swing when we got there with girls earnestly (like their lives depended on it in fact) listening to one another and boys leaning into the wall like ruffians. In the jacks we combed our hair and straightened our ties and fixed ourselves up in front of a huge uncomplimentary mirror. 'Who's the fairest of them all?' someone cried. Somebody else was spewing in one of the cubicles and a hardcase who was trying to steal his way in through a tiny window got caught red-handed by the tubby bouncer.

'What are you at there?' the bouncer bawled, hitching at his falling-down pants and scratching his hair-infested pot belly.

'What? I'm gettin' out,' the burglar piped, and sure enough back out he climbed.

At the foot of the stairs to the balcony a crowd of boys waited for their girls to come out of ***The Ladies***. Danny and I enviously watched some of these girls descending, their flimsy light dresses clinging without a bulge or a bump to their dainty virgin figures. And then they fell into each other's arms and sort of glided towards the dimly lit dance floor.

We made our way down through the hall, which was beginning to fill up now. We took in the relief band - Tommy Day And The Bandits, belting out *Boys* - and the corny waltzers who were already showing off out on the floor, and the girls, all bunched together around the shop, trying to avoid the famous maulers who were prowling the hall like Casanovas. Over in the darkest corner a wayward gang had formed, and sitting along the side walls were the sad faced fallen-out lovers and the shy people and the newcomers at their first dance. From the ceiling the silver ball dangled, spinning and speckling the hall with psychedelic beams of light, and every now and then the hand held spot on the balcony shone across the dancers like a searchlight.

The Freshmen opened that night with *Papa Oo Mow Mow* and then followed with The Hollies *On a Carousel*. After that they went straight into *Matthew and Son* with the expert brass section pounding and blasting, fading and reappearing again. Billy Brown was singing, thumping that old pumping Hammond organ, his head cocked sideways as he writhed and shaped stylishly, his beautiful nasal voice looming out over our heads. When they did a great version of *Night of Fear* Danny's head came up over the throng, acknowledging the fact that I knew my onions when it came to music and bands.

We were dancing with two girls now, two lovely girls with crisp new dresses on them and shining hair and soft, almost angelic faces. When the band slowed down I wrapped my arms around my partner and she snuggled in real close to me. The band were playing the slow-motion, surreal *Strawberry Fields Forever* and I had this lovely vision of a race of people whose language is music. These people dance their lives away with everything swirling perfectly. Even the fancy dancers don't get in anybody's way as they waltz and foxtrot and steer in and out of the maze of bodies, and even if they did bump into someone now and again nobody would mind. Unlike us they have rhythm you see, and they know that words and music and movement are the key…*Ba Ba Ba…*

When the song ended the girl smiled at me and said thanks for the dance and went back to her friend. I couldn't see Danny anywhere and so I went up to the front to watch the band for a while. Then I got a tip on the shoulder and I turned to find Kathy standing there. She told me that Danny was looking for me, that he was waiting for me down at the back of the hall. I knew by her face that something was up. Not even for a split second did I imagine that she wanted to dance with me. I hurried through the crowd and found him out in the foyer. He had already retrieved our coats from the cloakroom.

'What's wrong?' I asked, seeing his face drained of blood.

'Skeleton Delaney is just after tellin' me that The Shamrock is on fire,' he said, handing me my coat.

'On fire?'

'Yeah. The fire brigade is down there and everything.'

'Is it bad did he say?'

'He said the flames are touching the sky,' Danny told me sorrowfully.

Outside it was spitting rain. We turned our collars up and made a run for it, turning into Cinema Lane and onto the Quay. My heart pounded when I heard the bottles popping in the distance and saw the angry sparks juggling high above the rooftops. As soon as I turned that heartbreaking corner my knees almost buckled to see the raging fire ripping through the remains of the bar. The shooting flames hissed and crackled as plaster, beams and bricks came crashing down to earth with a dead hopeless thud. A crowd had already gathered and they gasped at the swiftness of it all - tired dancers who happened to be passing, people living close by and evacuated residents of The Small Hotel, which was also in danger. George was standing under the canopy and when he became aware of me he came my way. I got a terrible fright when one of the firemen asked me, 'Where's your da, Davy?' and for an awful moment I thought that maybe my father and mother were both inside.

'Aw no, they went up home alright, Davy,' George assured me and volunteered to go and get a loan of a car to drive me up to the house.

When my father opened up the front door I had to laugh with relief and he looked at the pair of us suspiciously, sensing something was up.

'She's gone aul' stock,' were the exact words that George used to break the news, and they were delivered so mournfully that my father didn't really need any more information. 'The whole lot is gone up in smoke,' George told him.

'What, my accordion and all,' my father said, obviously stunned.

'The whole shebang,' George sympathised.

'God, what am I goin' to do now?' my father uttered half to himself, giving a faint, fey grin, and his tossed sleepy head, his bristly chin where the sharp greyish hairs had already begun to sprout, and the surprised hurt in his eyes brought it all home to me.

'If you want a lift down there now or anything I'll hang on for you,' George offered.

'Naw, there's no point is there?' my father said, fixing his braces and scratching himself. 'If she's gone, she's gone,' he said.

'I suppose,' George agreed, and I watched the pair of them going down the hall towards the kitchen.

Upstairs the landing creaked and I looked up to see my mother standing above me.

'Were you down there, Davy?' she wondered.

'Yeah,' I said.

'And is it as bad as George was saying?'

I told her it was and then I closed the front door and followed the men down to the kitchen.

⁂

The next morning it was nothing but a smouldering wasteland of burnt-out debris: shattered bottles, the grey ashy frame of the counter, the wrecked black till, the skeleton of his old faithful accordion and the twanging shell of the piano; smoking foam and springs that coiled themselves around other things, singed photographs and scattered ashes that took flight to land in the vast sorry harbour; sad things piled up and moulded together as if trying to protect one another from the attacking heat, along with heaped mountains of unrecognisable articles which were still too hot to handle. The Small Hotel looked lost without its tipsy companion - no one to link or whisper her chandeliered secrets to. There was nothing left but a vacant space and a serenaded street that would never be the same again.

People stood around gabbing, some of them glad of the distraction, no doubt. Most of the boys showed up too, looking like embarrassed mourners at a funeral, moping around as if it was half their fault - Hickey and Joe Crofton and Forty Winks, Lar Lyons and Durango Clark; and Victor of course who kept the inquisitive children at bay. I was told that Victor later uncovered from beneath a red hot lump of foam an elegant novelty cigarette lighter which on request he'd proudly hold up to the light.

For me it was all over then I'm afraid, and in no time at all the boys vanished from my life like ghost ships in the night. All except Crunch that is, good old El Cruncho. He's still around - a walking, breathing Useless Island. I often happen on him, rambling up the Quay or stepping out of an alleyway or sitting on a high stool in some old shadowy back street bar. He has taken to wearing a hat these days and he uses a walking stick from time to time. I spied him the other day drinking in The Cape Of Good Hope, surrounded by a bunch of denim clad jokers. He was painting them a picture of Valparaiso and talking about Indio, running out of hands and words to describe her build. And when he glanced my way his mischievous grin invited me to relive it all again - the love and the loss and the pain, and that awful feeling of being alone for the first time in my life as I stood there, lost in the rain, watching the walls of The Shamrock come tumbling down.